A
Fatal
Development

Julie Kendrick

A Fatal Development

This is a work of fiction. Events and characters described herein are imaginary and are not intended to refer to specific places or living persons. The opinions expressed in this manuscript are solely the opinions of the author and do not represent the opinions or thoughts of the publisher. The author has represented and warranted full ownership and/or legal right to publish all materials in this book.

This book may not be reproduced, transmitted, or stored in whole or in part by any means, including graphic, electronic, or mechanical without the express written consent of the publisher except in the case of brief quotations embodied in critical articles and reviews.

Cover photo, *Red Pail,* © 2009 Kendrick Photographic Imagery

ISBN 978-0-9976262-0

Evil hiding among us is an ancient theme.

—John Carpenter

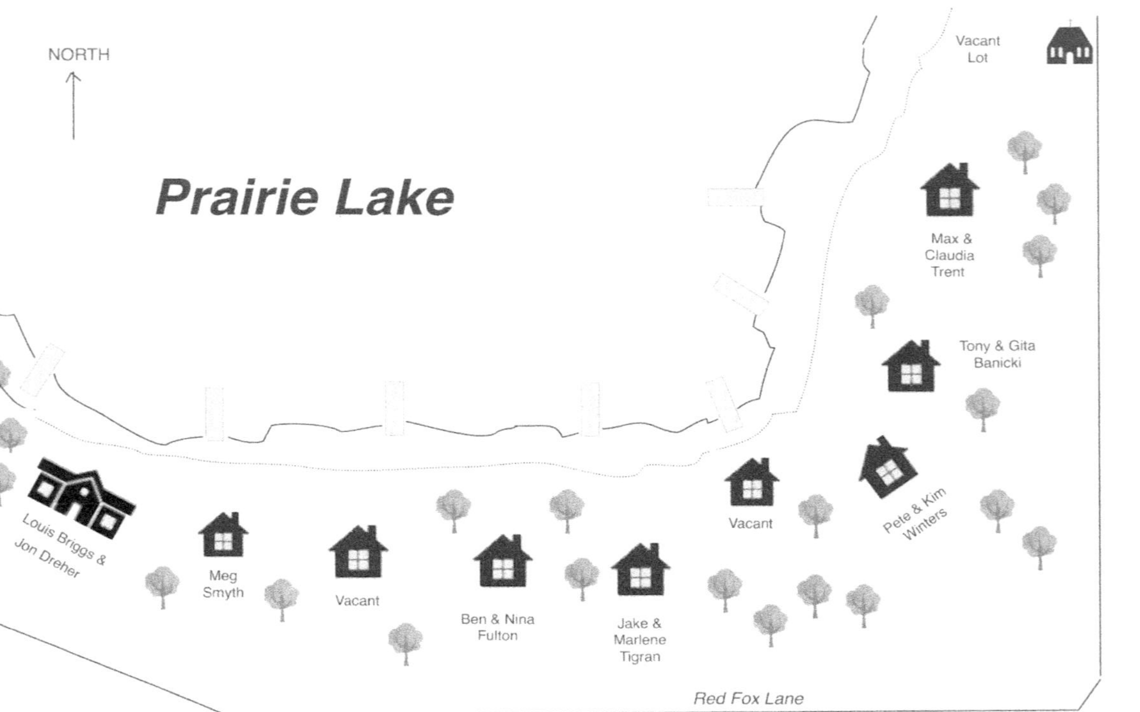

NORTH
Prairie Lake
Vacant Lot
Max & Claudia Trent
Tony & Gita Banicki
Pete & Kim Winters
Vacant
Louis Briggs & Jon Dreher
Meg Smyth
Vacant
Ben & Nina Fulton
Jake & Marlene Tigran
Red Fox Lane
"Cottage Row"

Chapter 1

The Statue of Liberty grinned and waved at me from the sidewalk. I smiled and waved back at him. Another marketing ploy for the Liberty Café was in full swing. Somehow, I felt I'd seen his costume before. Stopped for the red light, I leaned across the car seat, and asked from my open window, "Hi, Max! Where did you get the outfit?"

"I borrowed it from my tax guy. His company used it to attract customers at tax time."

Max Trent stood stolidly in the hot sun. His flowing electric-green robes added to his generous proportions, while the dark stubble on his chin and large black-rimmed glasses betrayed the gender of Lady Liberty. His spiked crown listed precariously over his left ear. Had I known the Statue was in such bad shape, I would've sent a donation to the Restoration Fund.

Max pointed to the sign next to him: "The Liberty Café—Where the Masses Huddle and Kids Eat Free."

"Good luck!" I called as the light changed and I drove off.

§

At moments like this, I knew why I love living in Bramble, a small town hugging the Wisconsin border and tucked beside Prairie Lake, carved out eons ago by retreating glaciers. Bramble. I laughed to myself. The founding fathers named the village in honor of the ornamental shrubs one of them planted around the town. The "bramble bushes" turned out to be buckthorns, a highly invasive species and bane of every homeowner.

I no longer try to explain why I abandoned my Chicago lifestyle. I occasionally miss walking down LaSalle Street at seven in the morning when the financial district throbs in preparation for another day; or watching the city lights wink in greeting to the descending night; or gazing from my condo at Lake Michigan in all its moods. Some days I even miss seeing my editor, Harry Josten.

But let's not get sappy about this. Harry knows I have no intention of trading my serenity for the stress of city living, and complains at least once a month about his martyrdom in dealing with me, living as I do in a land of slow Internet connections and three-day power outages. Oh well. My columns, if not always of Pulitzer caliber (okay, rarely), are filed on time, admittedly via overnight service more often than not. "You've never left me with an eight-column-inch hole in Sub Living," he often remarks, unable to resist adding an acid-tongued, "That's why I keep you, Miss Polly."

Miss Polly. That's me. Well, it's not me; it's my *nom de plume,* if such there be in today's journalism world. I am one of a long line of advice givers: Emily Post, Ann Landers, Miss Manners, Dear Abby. My column, "Miss Polly's Opinion," runs twice a week in the *Journal-Times,* and is syndicated in dozens of papers across the country. "Miss Polly" has even published two books. It isn't quite what I had in mind when I graduated from the Medill School of Journalism at Northwestern, but it's still mostly fun. It also keeps me from fulfilling my mother's dire prediction when I bought my first car—a bright red convertible: "Young lady, if you don't stop your spendthrift ways, you'll end up eating cat food." So far, only Minerva—my domestic shorthair with stunning green eyes and sleek black coat—dines on Meow Mix.

My real name is Margrethe Gae Smyth—Meg, for short. My mother's side of the family is descended from sturdy Danish stock, so naming me for Queen Margrethe seemed the thing to do. My middle name, Gae, I share with an aunt who still lives in Copenhagen. Dad managed to assert his English background when my brother, James Edward, was born.

The sultry air promised more humidity to come. As I pulled into a space in front of Ben's Hardware to pick up more grout to finish tiling my bathroom, I glanced at my hands on the steering wheel. They were red and raw, covered with tiny scratches from trimming ceramic tile. Death by a thousand cuts. The project was almost finished, except for a last bit of grouting. I rather enjoyed the measuring and shaping of tiles. Another hand-me-down from the Danes: Grampa Nielsen had been a bricklayer.

The bell over the door jingled as I entered. "Hi, Ben!" I called. Ben Fulton turned from the ladder where he was hoisting a large shipment of roofing nails onto a shelf. He climbed down and wiped his hands on his carpenter's apron. It was always bulging with nails, tape measure, washers, and other miscellaneous stuff, and was as much a part of him as the store itself. His father, nick-named (of course) Big Ben when baby Ben was born, died years ago, bequeathing the store to his only child, now middle-aged. As a toddler, so the local story goes, Ben amused his father's custom-ers by identifying various sizes of nuts and bolts.

Ben gave me a broad grin and brushed a damp wisp of gray hair back from his forehead. "Sure is hot for late September. How's your pro-ject coming?"

I told him I needed just a bit more grout. Ben set a small can of quick-drying, pre-mixed grout on the counter, then took a flat carpenter's pencil from his apron pocket and marked the cost on a slip of paper. He placed it and my money in a tin can, which his wife Nina pulleyed by wire to the balcony of the store where she sat at a small desk. Ben's Hardware had to be one of the few remaining stores on the planet with a can-and-pulley system to process credit cards and tally up cash sales. The soft ring of the old cash register as Nina pressed down the keys was homey and oddly reassuring. Her plump face crinkled in a smile, she looked down and waved to me as she returned the can to Ben.

Ben counted out the change—a retail art nearly lost to computerization—and wished me well as, over my protests, he slipped a small bottle of Corn Huskers Lotion into the sack.

§

I turned onto Red Fox Lane and pulled up at the little house my grandparents left me. It stands on a smallish lot on the lake shore, and is one of several cottages built along the lake in the 1930s as an artist retreat colony, which folded with the onset of World War Two. The nine homes still standing are known as "Cottage Row." Now, in 1998, two of them, including the one next door to mine, had been vacant for a long time and were marked by blistered paint and hanging gutters. Their curtainless windows stared at the lake with unseeing eyes.

Changing into my grubbies, I set to work, crawling around under the pedestal sink, grouting the tile on the wall around the pipes. Actually, I thought smugly, as I admired the fit of the ceramic, my tiling doesn't look too bad, considering the difficulty in shaping square tiles around round pipes. I imagined the oohs and aahs of my friends, and laughed aloud. Good grief, woman, get a grip. As if my friends would crawl around on the bathroom floor to admire my workmanship.

As with most jobs, this one took longer than I thought it would; the quick-drying grout wasn't so "quick" in the humid weather. Finally, I stood and stretched, gathered up my tools, and took them into the mudroom to clean. I looked inside my refrigerator, shuddered at the congealed pieces of leftover pizza, and avoided altogether inspecting gastronomical mysteries in plastic containers moldering into science projects. In view of my completed tiling project, a celebratory dinner was in order. By my definition, a celebratory dinner could not be cooked by me or it wouldn't be celebratory. I never understood the appeal of restaurants featuring home-cooked meals.

Right now, however, I smelled like a goat. I glanced into the mirror. My hair stood up in dirty clumps. Peeling off my sweaty shorts and tee shirt, I hopped into the shower. Well, maybe not exactly hopped. I was beginning to feel the results of an afternoon spent twisting and turning in the narrow confines under my sink. The old brass faucets squealed as I turned them. And turned them. The faucets went round and round, releasing only a pitiful stream of rusty water. I was too exhausted to cry.

I cleaned up as best I could at the sink, my face in the mirror showing every one of my lines and wrinkles. My mother's words came back to me from my youth: "Put on some make-up, Meg. You look like a blank page." Okay, Mom. I gave my lips a swipe of lipstick, applied a bit more blush, and finished off with generous sprays of toilet water. Why is it called toilet water? Sounds like something a dog would order as a pre-prandial canine cocktail. Enough.

I headed out the door, stopped. There was a sign in my front yard. Someone must have pounded it into the grass while I was inside working. I walked over and read, "Hearing scheduled on this property…"

About a year ago, a Chicago-based company, Porter-Burton Enterprises, PBE for short, obtained an option to purchase several hundred acres of property along the south end of Prairie Lake. The company planned to run in sewer lines, dredge and deepen the lake, and build sixty condominiums and town homes. Private boat slips for motor craft and a full-service marina were also part of the proposal. Adjoining the property, Cottage Row was an integral part of the plan. A number of residents formed a group to try to block construction of the proposed waterfront development.

My stomach knotted. I'd received registered letters with notices, attended meetings on the subject—now a sign in my yard. The Bramble village board was considering declaring Cottage Row "blighted" because of the long-term vacancies, seize it through the process of eminent domain, and sell it to developers. "More jobs for local people!" was the rallying cry of the board's supporters. Conversations about the possible development sizzled all summer in Bramble.

I yanked the sign from the ground and tossed it in the trashcan at the curb for pick up the next day.

§

The Heron, Bramble's upscale restaurant, offered a fresh-fish special every evening. Unusual side dishes and savory soups accompanied all entrées. Other than a couple of fast-food eateries out on the highway, for my festivities tonight it was either the Heron or the Liberty Café, home of the Belly Buster Burger and Lady Liberty. No contest. By the way, "upscale" is a relative term in Bramble. The Heron is considered a bit *la-di-da* by some of the locals due to its refusal to serve men wearing baseball caps while dining.

The Heron is owned and managed by Louis Briggs and Jon Dreher, a couple who moved in next door to me a few years ago. Although they are out, they remain circumspect with displays of their long-standing affection for each other. "Not everyone accepts gays," commented Jon to me one evening. No kidding.

Louis greeted me with a big hug. Jon presumably was in the kitchen overseeing food preparation. Dressed in knife-creased khakis, white shirt, and cordovan loafers polished to mirrored perfection, Louis showed me to a booth in a quiet corner. I gratefully sank into the cool leatherette seat, wincing a bit from my earlier activities. As he handed me the menu, Louis clucked over my red, scratched hands. A thought flitted through my mind of an old television commercial for hand cream that asked, "Would you hold hands with a cactus?" That's me: the town saguaro.

I chose the Alaskan salmon special, accompanied by a chilled cucumber and leek soup, rice pilaf, and asparagus tips served chilled with a chervil cream sauce. I ordered a glass of Chablis to keep me company while I waited for my food.

Louis soon brought out the meal. I dug into the food like a longshoreman after a tough day on the wharf. Preoccupied with the joy of someone else's cooking, I ignored thoughts of the lake development clamoring for my attention.

I didn't notice the voices across the room until they were loud enough to intrude on my enjoyment of my wonderful meal. "Our house has been in the family for years. Used to come out here to visit my granny, swim and fish, when I was a kid. Now my kids are growing up here. They know how to sail, ice-skate, the schools are good. I'm not givin' up my home!

"All you and Travis Burton want is to make a quick buck and go on to the next place to spoil with your heavy equipment and overpriced houses. Now you're trying to get the village board behind you. You're all crooks!"

I glanced over, although I recognized the strident voice without looking. Pete Winters. Pete's company, Pump N Dump, serviced most, if not all of the septic systems along the lake. With the development, a sewer system would replace them. His long braid hung below his shoulders and swung to and fro in accompaniment to his animated tirade. In a kinder and bygone world, Pete's physique might be described as portly. His belly extended over the table where Simon Porter, one of the partners of Porter-Burton Enterprises, was eating.

Porter eyed the vast tummy sharing his table linens. Not turning a hair of what must be a seventy-five-dollar haircut, he reached for his glass of water. "And you are…oh, yes. The um…sanitary system guy." He wrinkled his nose.

"You can try to belittle an honest trades-man," Winters replied. "but don't think that you and PBE can just come in here and ruin our town. We have ways of dealing with vultures like you!" He strode off. As he tried to slam the door, the door-closer hardware whispered it shut. As Porter turned back to his meal, a smile touched the corner of his mouth.

I sighed and continued eating.

"Mind if I join you?" I looked up as my friend, Sally Montrose, slid into the seat across from me.

I smiled. "Please do."

"Craig's sequestered with some project, so I thought I'd run an errand or two. Saw your car in the parking lot." Fluent in several languages, Sally's husband works from home as an investment adviser for a number of companies with overseas clients.

"How did the reading at the lake go today?" I inquired. Although childless after several years of marriage, Sally is a favorite among the youngsters and thinks up creative ways to interest kids in reading. This week was the last of this year's "Stories on the Beach," read-aloud storytimes for toddlers at the public lakeside park. The young mothers in Bramble love the program; after the stories, a sack lunch, and fresh air, their children are ready for a long afternoon nap.

"You mean the traumatic reading. The kids seem to have so much trouble paying attention to the story. Maybe it's too much television. Or," she added, "perhaps I'm just getting older."

"Well, you don't look the worse for wear." Of course she didn't. Sally would look clean, refreshed, and well put-together after cleaning latrines.

Tall and slim, Sally has subtly tinted blonde hair drawn back, every strand held in place with a black ribbon. Miss Clairol helps me get in touch with my roots; Sally goes to a colorist. Sally works part-time at the Bramble Library and was among the first people I met when I moved here. Our mutual interest in books led us to become good friends from the first time I visited the library to research something for my newspaper column.

She and Craig have lived in Bramble for nearly ten years and are renovating an old Victorian house in town—a project that never seems to end.

I asked, "How's the house?"

"Not so good. The basement is damp, and we're afraid mold will start to grow in Craig's office, so we're going to have it waterproofed and add a sump pump. They're going to dig a drainage trench around part of the foundation, so landscaping will need to wait."

"Sounds serious."

"We've put it off until now, what with all the other work we've done on the house. In any case, water's not good for the foundation. It has to be done, but it's so much more fun to paint, wallpaper, or hunt for antique furniture."

"Yeah. It's not very exciting to invite people to see a new sump pump," I agreed. Uninvited, the vision of guests creeping along my bathroom floor to admire the tiling flashed through my mind.

"You're right!" Sally said.

Startled from my reverie, I stared at her.

"Craig and I should invite some people over soon."

"To admire your sump pump?"

Sally laughed. "We can have the party before we tear up the yard. The main floor is finished, so…"

We looked up as Louis bustled over with a menu.

Sally waved it away. "I had a late lunch, thank you, Louis. Just a glass of your house merlot."

"I'll have another Chablis, Louis," I said.

Sally glanced at my empty wine glass, then at me. I rarely indulged in a second glass. "Here I've been prattling on about the house, and you look upset, Meg. What's up?"

I told her about the sign in my front yard. "Pete Winters is determined to stop the development. He was in here earlier raging at Simon Porter." I toyed with my empty wine glass. "I feel like raging, too. I love the quiet, the slower pace of life here. Prairie Lake is too small for motorized boats and those awful Sea-doo things buzzing around the lake. Why would people think that's fun?"

"Beats me," Sally replied, as Louis arrived with our wine.

"Seriously, Sally, this can't be allowed to happen."

"I know. The development will affect all of us—not just Cottage Row."

"Want to go with me to the hearing tomorrow night?"

"Absolutely."

We chatted a while longer before leaving the restaurant together. Sally gave me a hug. "See you tomorrow!"

The night welcomed me home like a soft blanket. The air was lush and crickets chirped in the marsh grass rustling on the shore as the water slapped quietly against the dock. A thumbnail moon bathed the lake in tiny ripples of silver. I gazed up at the starry sky and listened to the night sounds a long while before going inside.

Chapter 2

Sporting his trademark red cap and bib overalls, Jake Tigran, the local plumber who lives with his family in a cottage down the road from me, arrived the next morning to fix my bathroom shower faucets. He looked around. "Been doing some tiling, have you?"

"Yes."

"Hmm."

Hmm? That's all he has to say about my tiling? I sighed. It's not easy being the Marc Chagall of bathroom tile.

Jake wrapped a rag around his wrench. "Don't want to scratch these fittings. Can't hardly find real brass hardware anymore," he said, shifting a plug of tobacco from one cheek to another. "These old brass fixtures just need some washers, and they'll be good as new."

"Great!" Hoping he wouldn't use my shower as a spittoon, I headed downstairs to the kitchen. After pouring myself a cup of coffee, I sat at the table where Minerva was curled up in my inbox with most of her hindquarters hanging over the edge. She watched me through slitted eyes, then resumed her nap. I opened my laptop and began sorting through e-mails. Amazing how many people wanted to enhance my sex life or invest their deceased uncle's fortune in my bank account. I worked steadily all morning on my next Miss Polly column until Jake called from the bathroom, "Come up and take a look!"

I admired the faucets and paid him. As he was leaving, I asked, "You going to the meeting tonight?"

Jake replied, "Sure am! PBE's going to hire a lot of local contractors. I figure with the money from selling them my house, and the extra work, I can move into town. Or even move away from here. Our house is too small for Marlene and me and three kids."

I said nothing. My house is my sanctuary. I feel safe here after living in Chicago. I can walk anywhere at night and not feel I have to look over my shoulder.

Jake headed for the door. "I'll see you tonight."

§

Back to business. I opened an envelope of mail forwarded from the newspaper. Despite having a laptop computer, I still found it faster to organize my thoughts by jotting notes on yellow legal pads I kept for that purpose. Most letters to Miss Polly were from distressed readers, primarily women, who sought an opinion from Miss Polly. Sometimes it was easy to dash off a witty reply. Not today. It seemed every writer had issues requiring more than a few light sentences. One was from a woman physically abused by her husband; another from a terminally ill patient who suspected her caregiver was poisoning her. I urged them to contact a counselor or the police or at least, confide in a friend. I found it difficult to concentrate, as thoughts of their plights mingled with thoughts of the possibility of losing my home. By mid-afternoon, I finally finished my column, sent it off to Harry, and closed my laptop.

I could clean out my clothes closet. I got up from the kitchen table, stretched, and walked upstairs. Pulling open the door to the closet, I scanned the forgotten items hanging in forlorn ranks: some of them from another era, others from another (smaller) size. I closed the door. Not today.

I puttered around the house a bit more. After a dinner of leftovers from last night's meal at the Heron, I changed out of my faded college tee shirt and cut-off jeans, and drove to meet Sally at the Bramble Town Hall. The meeting was scheduled early, 6:30 p.m., to avoid conflict with Bramble High School's football game against the Walnut Creek Hawks.

§

The Bramble Town Hall lot was almost full—a big turnout for what the *Bramble Buzz,* our local weekly, termed "The Clash of the Titans." Hyperbole run riot. I squeezed my car into a spot near the back of the lot.

Built about fifty years ago, the Town Hall had undergone several additions, the most recent one cobbled on after a tornado ripped through the area several years ago. The result was a drab building of indeterminate style. However, the interior of the town hall retained vestiges of Art Deco in the overhead chandeliers of art glass, the brushed nickel fixtures wasting their glow on rows of institutional folding chairs on the floor below them. At the front of the room stood a small platform containing a table and several mismatched chairs where our village trustees plunked down their bottoms during board meetings. A podium with a microphone was to one side. So far, the stage was empty.

"Meg!" Sally called to me from the third row where her coat was draped over the empty seat next to her.

"Hi, Sally," I said. I shrugged off my light jacket. "Quite a crowd tonight. Parking lot's almost full. Craig coming?"

"Maybe later. He's home on the phone with someone halfway around the world. A lot of his clients are in other countries and he often works during their business hours."

We stood and gazed around the room. Louis Briggs was talking with Ben and Nina Fulton, her wheelchair tucked in next to the center aisle. Max Trent, *sans* his Lady Liberty robes, sat several rows behind them with Tony Banicki, who lived with his invalid mother in Cottage Row. Pastor Joe Jenkins, his cherubic face serious above his clerical collar, was deep in conversation with Jake Tigran next to him. Pete Winters glared around the room from his seat at the far end of the front row.

At the other end of the front row near the stage, Bramble Police Chief Billy Koenig, his torso straining the buttons on his uniform shirt, surveyed the room. Seated with him were four men. One was an elderly gentleman with wispy white hair, a hawkish nose, and a deeply lined face. Next to him was a man who had a full head of dark hair, and the same prominent nose of the older man. I guessed he was Edwin Porter, his son Simon next to him. With them was another man, well built with dark brown eyes. From the brochures that wedged in our front doors almost weekly, I recognized Travis Burton. Another man, tall, with wavy auburn hair wasted on a male of our species, took the last seat next to them.

"The old guy must be Edwin Porter, Simon's father," I said to Sally. "And I recognize Travis Burton from all the literature they've distributed. But who's that next to them?"

She shrugged. "Haven't any idea. He's kinda cute, though." She gave me a significant look. Always the matchmaker, our Sally.

Fred Koenig, Chief Koenig's older brother, labored up the stairs to the podium. Jovial and beefy, he had served as Bramble's mayor since Woodrow Wilson was in the White House. Okay, maybe not that long, but for many years. Fred's attire reflected the importance of the meeting: he wore a tie. He lumbered up to the podium and blew into the microphone to test it. I cringed. Why don't people just say, "Testing, testing?" As if it were in sync with my thoughts, the mike squealed.

"Good evening, folks," Fred began. He beamed at the crowd. Silence greeted him. His smile curdled and he hurried on. "We're pleased to have representatives from PBE, who'll address concerns you might have about their plans for Prairie Lake." The mayor started to clap as the Simon Porter and Travis Burton mounted the stairs, but stopped when no one else joined in. Fred turned and sat in one of the chairs on the stage.

The two men walked across the stage and stood shoulder to shoulder at the podium. "Good evening," said Porter. "Before we begin, I'd like to introduce my father, Edwin Porter." He gestured to the elderly man in the front row, who wore a dark suit and a tie knotted in an old-fashioned Windsor. Gold cufflinks gleamed from his sleeves. The man stood briefly and nodded to the crowd.

Simon Porter continued. "My partner, here, and I look forward to addressing some of your concerns—either tonight or one-on-one at your convenience—about our plans for the improvement of the waterfront at the south end of Prairie Lake."

"Some improvement!" called out Pete Winters.

Burton stepped forward, "The waterfront homes are only part of the picture, as you know. The quality of the lake will be much improved. We'll dredge and deepen that end, so you can have bigger watercraft—even, powerboats—for fishing. No more sitting in an uncomfortable row boat or canoe." Burton added with a smirk, "Unless you want to, of course." He looked expectantly at the audience. Silence.

Porter edged in front of Burton and filled the silence. "Best of all, we'll employ over a hundred local workers to help with the lake development and build the homes on the shore."

Applause. Everyone's heads turned to see Max Trent and Jake Tigran clapping vigorously. Several people booed.

"They're not taking my home!" Heads swiveled again. Pete Winters, red-faced, glowered from his seat up front.

"You can move somewhere else," shouted Max. "They've offered to buy our houses…"

"Thieves! Crooks!" Pete Winters was on his feet. "Fair price? Hardly!"

More shouts. "These are our families' homes!" "We've lived here for generations!"

"Please, please! Let's keep calm." The voice of Pastor Joe rang out.

"Listen," replied Porter. He gestured in Max's direction. "Mr. Trent is right. We'll give you good money for your homes. We're working with your elected officials to help raze those old, empty houses. They're eyesores, a blight on your lovely community. In their place, we…"

More angry voices ripped the air. Mayor Koenig walked to the podium, raised his hands for quiet. "Now, folks, you know the village government is considering eminent domain, acquiring the properties for a public marina, maybe." The crowd erupted in a cacophony of jeers and applause, all but drowning out Koenig, as he shouted, "We'd rather not do things that way, of course…"

Sally leaned toward me. "This is getting dangerous." She was right. The assembly was beyond restless. Winters stood, turned to the crowd, and led them in chanting, "Save our lake! Save our lake!"

Mayor Koenig escorted the developers from the stage and out a side door.

§

The crowd streamed from the building. A small group formed in the parking lot around Pete and Jake who began to shove each other. Chief Koenig quickly stepped in and, wrapping an arm around Jake's shoulder, led him off to where his truck was parked.

"Wow. I've never seen anything like that. What do you think will happen?" Sally asked.

"Looks like Mayor Koenig, the village board, and the developers are going to push the development over Pete and his group's protests," I answered.

"We'll do more than just protest, Meg," a masculine voice said. "A lot more."

Sally and I jumped. Neither of us had noticed Pete Winters come up behind us. His hands were clenched in tight balls as he strode past us to his truck and sped away.

§

Sally's car was parked nearby. After we hugged, I headed for the dark corner of the lot where I had left my car. The crowd had dispersed. My automobile seemed miles away. Why didn't I ask someone to walk me to my car? I shook off my anxiety for a moment, until, as I half-trotted to my car, I remembered a magazine article I browsed in the supermarket checkout line. Some cop or Army ranger or black-belt type had written an article about how women can defend themselves against attack. I could recall only one of his points: be aware of your surroundings.

I was aware all right. Especially when the parking lot lights went out. I stood motionless while my eyes adjusted to the abrupt darkness. I could hear leaves rustling in the trees. Just leaves, I reassured myself. A puff of breeze and the hairs on my neck rose in response. I hurried on. A few more feet to reach the safety of my car.

More of the magazine article came back to me. I gripped my keys so they pointed outward, so I could attack a mugger's eyes. I readied myself for a few kicks to his kneecaps and groin. I didn't feel any safer. I reached my car and fumbled with the lock. My keys dropped to the ground. My next car will have electronic door openers, I vowed.

"Need some help?"

I cried out.

"I'm sorry to frighten you."

Frighten me? I was terrified. I wheeled around and gazed into the face of the stranger sitting with the Porter-Burton group.

"I was leaving, and saw you walking over here in the dark. Thought I'd stick around and make sure you got out of here safely." He stooped, picked up my keys, and handed them to me.

"Th-thank you," I said shakily. I turned the key in the lock. "I'll be okay."

"Are you sure? I feel badly about scaring you. I'm Brad Trinder, by the way. Our car is right over here," he said, pointing to large car parked several feet away. "We're heading back to the hotel in town, but I'll watch until you're safely out of the lot."

"Thank you again," I said, getting into my car. I felt foolish, having let my imagination run wild. What next? Goblins under my bed? I didn't realize how tense I was until I entered my house and closed the door behind me.

Chapter 3

After a restless night, I woke to Minerva kneading my shoulder. How can a small cat feel so heavy? She stared into my eyes, a purr rumbling in her throat. I scratched her under her chin, rolled out of bed, and padded into the bathroom. I thought about the incident in the parking lot last night, and laughed to myself. My imagination was both a blessing and a curse.

As I twirled my toothbrush over my molars, I planned a day of work. Maybe I'd even surprise Harry with my next column. My intentions were sincere, but after nearly an hour of chewing my pencil as I shuffled through my notes, twisting my hair, and staring at my computer, I gave up. Besides, Harry was not getting any younger and might suffer a shock if my next Miss Polly column arrived early.

I drove into town, slipped the car into a spot on the street, and walked across the street to Norton's Drug and Sundries for an early lunch. Norton's is a throwback to a simpler time. In addition to the pharmacy and a few aisles of items ranging from pantyhose to homemade persimmon jam, Norton's offers breakfast and lunch. At the rear of the store were three booths. A dozen round chrome stools covered with cracked green vinyl are bolted to the floor in front of a counter. A simple food menu is available, along with a variety of fountain drinks such as Green River, cherry phosphates, thick shakes, and malted milks.

Two men sat at the counter. The mirror in back of the counter reflected their faces: Pastor Joe and the stranger who was at last night's meeting.

Both men swiveled toward me as I climbed onto the stool next to them. "Hi, Pastor Joe." Turning to the other man, I said. "Hi. Brad, right?"

"Yep. And you're…"

"Meg Smyth. Just call me Meg."

Brad Trinder picked up his menu and studied it while I studied him. He had a strong, angular face beneath the thick auburn hair I'd noticed the previous evening. I noted a sprinkling of gray hairs that weren't visible to me in the dark last night.

I pulled myself away from further contemplation of his anatomy as Pastor Joe said, "The development may turn out to be the godsend that the backers forecast, but Bramble is being polarized by it. Someone sprayed graffiti on the Porter-Burton construction trailer a few days ago. And the uproar at last night's meeting..." His eyebrows drew together in a frown. "No wonder greed is one of the seven deadly sins." He sighed, and perused his menu.

Unwilling to let go of the topic, I turned to Trinder. "You're a brave soul to come into this situation."

"Simon, Travis, and I are meeting with Pete Winters this afternoon," he said.

Before I could ask what Trinder's relationship was with PBE, Pastor Joe turned the conversation to less controversial topics, launching into an enthusiastic, if rambling, account of the upcoming church rummage sale. A young boy in an apron came through the swinging doors from the kitchen, and sauntered over to take our orders.

I resumed my conversation with Trinder. "What is it you do—?" I began.

There was a commotion in the front of the store. Looking into the mirror, I saw Jake gesturing wildly at the cashier. Her hands flew to her mouth, her eyes widened in horror. Seeing us, Jake hurried over. "There's been an accident! Simon Porter's been run over by a backhoe!"

"Oh no!" Pastor Joe grabbed Jake's sleeve. "Are you sure?"

"I was driving by and saw the police arrive at the Porter-Burton trailer, so I stopped. They wouldn't let me get very close, but I did see Porter's body in the shovel."

"How awful!" I said.

"I should be there in case there's something I can do." Pastor Joe turned to me, "Can you give me a lift? I walked here from the parsonage."

"Certainly."

"Mind if I tag along?" asked Trinder.

I shrugged. "Okay."

Trinder took out his wallet and tossed some bills on the counter, and we hurried out.

Chapter 4

We pulled up next to the county coroner's van where two technicians struggled to remove a gurney from the back of the vehicle. I grabbed the notebook and trusty Instamatic camera I always kept in the glove box—a throwback to my reporting days before Miss Polly. Pastor Joe held the door for him as Trinder slowly uncurled his tall, lanky frame from my back seat.

I looked around. When it first began contacting Bramble residents about the development of Prairie Lake, PBE rented the property, previously a lumberyard. They stored some of its construction equipment while the details of the Prairie Lake development were worked out. The construction office trailer was dark and empty. Lighter patches here and there where the siding had been scrubbed didn't quite obliterate the spray-painted graffiti. A forklift was parked near the steps and several massive earth-moving vehicles were lined up in orderly rows along the side. The lake shimmered in the distance beyond some scrubby bushes and tall weeds.

Trinder trailed behind Pastor Joe and me as we walked over to Chief Koenig, who stood talking with Jim Dowd, the county coroner. On the ground behind them, a rubberized sheet covered what presumably was Porter's body, part in, part out of the loader of an enormous orange backhoe. Yellow tape marked off the scene. I had only seen photos of Dowd when he ran for election, so I was surprised to see him in a polo shirt and jeans. You twit, Meg. Did you think he runs around in a lab jacket? Besides, it's Saturday. Probably missing his golf game.

The two men turned as we trooped over to them. "Hello, Pastor," Koenig said. He glared at me. "And what are you doing here, little lady?"

I gritted my teeth. "I'm here on assignment from the *Journal-Times.*" I wasn't, of course, but Koenig didn't need to know that. I'd square it with Harry later.

"Oh, great. A newspaper reporter." The Chief appeared to grit his teeth.

As we gritted, Dowd spoke up. "My office will have a statement later today. For now, we are calling Mr. Porter's death by undetermined cause. Come by around five o'clock today. We'll know more then."

I took out my camera and snapped a few photos—a task encumbered by the Chief's desire to strike a commanding pose, and Dowd's aversion to being photographed in casual clothes. The photos completed, I looked around for Trinder and spotted him as he ducked under the crime-scene tape and started toward us. Dowd and Koenig followed my glance.

"Hey!" shouted the Chief. "You can't be in there!"

"Sorry," Trinder said, looking abashed. "I didn't disturb anything." He walked over to us. "Chief, you might wish to consider how Simon got here. I don't see a car that doesn't belong to you or the coroner's office."

Billy's expression told all of us that this item had escaped him. "Already on it," said Billy.

The three of us climbed into my car. As we drove back to town, I said over my shoulder to Trinder, "I can't believe you crossed into the crime scene. Did you see anything?"

"I looked under the sheet. Porter wasn't run over by the backhoe. He was shot."

Chapter 5

"Shot!" Pastor Joe and I exclaimed in unison.

"At least one bullet in the chest," replied Trinder.

"But how can that be?" I asked. "Jake said Porter was run over."

"Jake only saw the body from the road. Probably jumped to that conclusion from the proximity of the backhoe." Trinder paused. "There's a good chance that after Porter was shot, the killer staged the body."

"Staged?" Pastor Joe asked.

"Quite a feat to shoot someone and have his body fall neatly in the backhoe shovel," Trinder replied.

"But why?"

Before Trinder could reply, I got it. "To send a message about the development!"

We rode in silence the rest of the way into Bramble, where I dropped Pastor Joe and Trinder back at Norton's and drove on home. It was only one o'clock, so I had some time to kill before heading over to the county coroner's office. *Time to kill.* The trite expression seemed ominous now.

I sent a short message about the murder to the paper. Harry telephoned and said he'd hold a hole on page four for additional information after I met with the coroner. I felt an unexpected rush. Guess I missed news reporting more than I realized. I headed out for Dowd's office in Walnut Creek, the county seat.

§

The county medical building is part of the oddly and euphemistically named "Seminole County Campus." Odd because the Seminoles never lived anywhere near here. Euphemistic because the mismatched buildings huddled together around the courthouse bear no resemblance whatever to ivy-covered halls of learning.

I pulled into the parking lot serving the county medical offices and forensic lab. Glass and aluminum structures were added onto the original redbrick building as needs and tax dollars—not necessarily in that order—permitted. Tired shrubs drooped around the border of the cracked asphalt.

A blast of air-conditioning greeted me as I entered the building. In response to my question, the security guard at the desk glanced up from *Field and Stream,* and pointed toward Jim Dowd's office. I hadn't been in the building before. A spidery web of dimly lit hallways spun off from the entrance area. The walls were painted in the nasty shades of olive drab I recalled from my youth in Chicago public schools. My footsteps echoed as I headed down the hall.

Entering the door marked "Seminole County Coroner," I stepped onto what felt like ankle-deep pile carpet. Dominating the small anteroom was a portrait of Coroner Dowd, his handsome face looking off into the distance as if contemplating an historic forensic pronouncement. Had taxpayer money popped for all this?

At the counter under the enormous painting, the receptionist held her voluminous purse in her hand, evidently ready to leave for the day. She motioned me to the chairs along one wall. "Dr. Dowd's in the lab. I've buzzed him. He'll be with you in a moment."

Before I had a chance to sit down, a door opened and Dowd strode in. This time, a white lab coat covered his pink golf shirt. He was drying his hands on a small towel. I tried not to think about where his hands had been.

"Hello," he said. "Please sit down, Ms…"

"Smyth."

"Oh, yes. A reporter with the *Journal-Times,* I believe."

"Right." There was no need for him to know that I usually was Miss Polly, advisor to the heartbroken. I took out my notebook and pencil.

Dowd handed me a sheet of paper. "Porter's family has been notified, so it's okay to identify him in your story." He nodded at the paper. "Here's a summary of our findings. Cause of death was a single bullet to the chest. It hit the aorta. We estimate the time of death between nine and ten last night.

"Was he killed where he was found?"

"Not exactly. There would've been more blood on the ground with a wound like that. His body was probably placed in the shovel postmortem," replied Dowd. "The forensics team found attempts to clean up a lot of blood in the trailer. Until we know for sure, please don't include that in your story."

We talked a while longer. Dowd shook my hand. I tried not to recoil. Moist and limp. Halibut hands. I restrained myself from wiping my hands on my pants until I was out of the building.

The warmth of the sun making its lingering farewell for the day felt comforting after the chill of the coroner's office.

Chapter 6

Dressed in flip-flops and a bathrobe covered with cat hair, I located the Sunday *Chicago Journal-Times* in one of the juniper bushes halfway down the driveway. Bramble is probably one of the last places on earth where an actual paperboy on a bike delivers the morning newspaper. He was not always accurate in his throw, but he was reliable. The paper usually arrived by six each morning.

My story on the Bramble murder led page four, with seven column-inches and a photo. Not bad for a non-Chicago murder. Harry had added some background information to my story, along with a file photo of Simon Porter and his wife at some posh North Shore society function.

I scanned down the page. Porter-Burton Enterprises had been formed late in the 1950s by Henry Burton and Edwin Porter. Burton had died a few years ago, leaving his share of the business to his son, Travis. When the elder Porter retired from active management of PBE recently, his son Simon moved up to partner with Travis Burton. I made a note to ask Harry to send more information about PBE from the paper's microfiche morgue.

Minerva in my lap and a second cup of coffee in hand, I learned that the Cubs lost the third and final game in the playoffs to Atlanta. We never should've traded Greg Maddux to the Braves. In the long-suffering Cubs fan tradition, I mumbled, "Wait 'til next year," and put the paper down. Time to get dressed for church.

The Bramble Evangelical Lutheran Church was about a fifteen-minute walk from my house. The older part of the church was built of native stone dredged from the lake. Two small stained-glass windows flanked the double doors leading into the sanctuary. The newer portion, containing the Sunday school and two or three meeting rooms, was frame, painted in neutral beige. To one side was a small cemetery. Some of the headstones dated back to the late 1800s, decades before Bramble was incorporated. Like broken teeth, many of the tombstones were askew. The church property abutted the property line of a vacant lot at one end of Cottage Row.

Pastor Joe was in rare form that morning, focusing on greed for his sermon topic. I looked around and saw several parishioners nodding in agreement with his words. I didn't need a degree in advanced psychology to figure out what was on their minds.

§

The next morning, I headed into town. The Bramble police station isn't imposing, lodged as it is in an old frame house. In addition to the police chief, we employ four full-time and two part-time police officers. Chief Koenig once tried to hire his wife as a matron, but the village board balked, citing the paucity of women offenders. The chief's squad car, one of three the village owns, was parked in the driveway. I went inside.

I waved to the young police officer at the desk and headed down the short hallway to where Ella Chapin, the Chief's receptionist, sat. "Hi, Ella. I'm here to see Chief Koenig."

Ella, her mouse-colored hair sprayed into an elaborate and impenetrable helmet, never looked up from her computer solitaire game. She gestured in the direction of the chief's office.

Billy Koenig's door was open and he beckoned me in. An air-conditioner rattled ineffectually in the window behind him. Beefy and florid-faced, Koenig smiled. "Hiya, Meg. What can I do ya for?"

I sighed inwardly. The good ol' boy greeting set my teeth on edge. I resigned myself to more gritting.

"I'm following up with you about the Simon Porter murder."

"Sure, honey. What would you like to know?" I scowled at him. Honey, indeed.

"Any new developments? Suspects? Motives?" I poised my pencil over my note pad. Koenig wiped his forehead and steepled his hands. A picture of sweaty thoughtfulness. "We're questioning everyone who was at the meeting the other night. The Prairie Lake plans have stirred up folks. Never seen anything like the hubbub around town."

"What about Pete Winters? Is he…?" I pressed. I doubted he would give out details, but if you don't ask, the answer's always no.

"Now, now. You know I can't talk about an ongoing investigation," Koenig said. "But tell you what. Drop by in a day or two and maybe we'll have something then."

He plodded over, placed a hammy paw on my back, and ushered me out the door.

Well, *honey,* that went well. I burned. I straightened my shoulders. I am not a Barbie doll. I am more than Miss Polly. I am a trained journalist. An investigative reporter. And it's time to in-investigate.

Chapter 7

As I drove home, thoughts swirled and eddied in my mind. A wave of doubt rolled over me. Could I really do investigative work again? Did I really want to?

My hands trembled on the steering wheel. Memories of my years scrabbling up the newspapering career tree slammed into me. Serving time on the city desk, taking feeds from reporters in the field, and monitoring the police scanner. Promoted to writing news briefs and covering somnolent city committee meetings and hearings. Eventually, I researched major stories, and reached the coveted position of a crime reporter.

Harry! I needed to bounce my return to investigative reporting off him. I let myself into the house, put down some food for Minerva, and glanced at the clock. Tomorrow's edition should be on the presses by now. Taking a deep breath, I lifted the phone and punched in Harry's direct number. He answered on the first ring.

"*Chicago Journal-Times.* Harry Josten."

"Hi, Harry, it's me, Meg Smyth.

"Hey, Meg. Some excitement in that peaceful village you live in, I see."

"Not so peaceful right now. Um…Harry, what would you think about me looking deeper into the murder here in Bramble?"

"Looking deeper? You mean like, investigating?"

"Yeah."

"Are you sure you want to do that, Meg? After that, um…I'd hate to have you hurt again…" His voice trailed off. A cavernous silence ensued as I struggled with my emotions.

"I know. I'm rather surprised at myself."

"Don't get me wrong. It'd be great to have you back," he said. "Simon Porter was well connected here in the city, so I was thinking of sending someone to Bramble to have a look around. But, Meg…"

"I have several evergreen Miss Polly columns filed."

"I know. I always appreciate having columns to run while you're on vacation or ill." He attempted a light remark. "Or if your Internet service is down out there in the sticks."

Another pause. "That's not the point," he continued. "I'm concerned about you, Meg. Tell you what. Send me a few 'graphs on what you've found out about the murder so far, okay? As far as continuing after that, why don't you sleep on it and call me tomorrow?"

"Harry…"

"Tomorrow, Meg."

We said good-bye. I placed the phone in its cradle. Harry was right. I needed to think some more about probing the murder. Under Minerva's watchful eye, I made a tuna salad sandwich, poured myself a glass of wine, and settled in on the living-room couch. I closed my eyes and thought back to my last days in Chicago.

§

Heading a task force consisting of three young reporters was my first major assignment. The four of us spent weeks working late in the newsroom, eating slabs of cold pizza washed down with warm soft drinks as we labored to peel back layers of corruption—bribes, kick-backs, pay-offs, extortion—connected with Chicago's Deep Tunnel project. Work on the Deep Tunnel system began in 1975, with work expecting to take more than fifty years to complete and a tab of billions of dollars. The massive civil engineering plan would decrease flooding in metro Chicago and reduce the amount of raw sewage flushed into Lake Michigan. Graft opportunities were, and probably still are rampant. There's never a shortage of crooks, racketeers, and money-grubbers in Chicago.

After intensive scrutiny by the newspaper's legal department, our multi-part story ran for several days under my byline, with "contributed by" credits to the other three on the task force. Wire services picked it up, and praise and congratulations came in from journalists all over the country. Shouts of, "Hey, Meg! Pulitzer Prize coming your way!" and "Way to go, Meg!" dominated the newsroom. I smiled. And yes, I preened. Recognition from one's peers is a heady experience.

Not surprisingly, calls from readers overwhelmed the *Journal-Times* switchboard. TV newscasters clamored for more information. Irate politicians took every opportunity to lambaste the paper and its management. Public uproar and circulation increased with each installment of our story.

Then the excitement turned sinister. My home phone rang late one night and a voice rasped, "You made a big mistake, Miss Snoop." It was the first of many threatening calls. I changed my phone number and kept it unlisted, but to no avail. Sometimes it was the rough voice detailing what he planned for me, other times just heavy breathing. I contacted the police, but they said there was nothing they could do except increase the number of times a patrol car cruised my neighborhood.

I lived in an older condominium off Michigan Avenue. It had a view of the lake if you craned your neck a bit, a fabulous kitchen largely unused by me, and a parking space under the building. I had another deadbolt installed on my door, and always carried pepper spray with me.

Unless I was chasing a story, I gave my elderly neighbor, Alfreda, a ride to the grocery store almost every Saturday. We often took a side trip to the Polish deli, where Alfreda, a native of Warsaw and survivor of a Nazi concentration camp, pointed out the various offerings. "Yah, Meggie, you must try dis," she'd say. And I usually did, to my delight.

Returning from one of our shopping outings, we laughed and chattered as I pulled into my parking spot under our apartment building. I woke up in Northwestern Memorial Hospital. A bomb had exploded near my car. I sustained a hairline skull fracture. Alfreda's aged heart could not survive the concussion from the blast. She died in the ambulance.

I recovered physically and returned to my condo, but Alfreda was always close to the surface of my thoughts. The bomber was never identified. The late-night phone calls continued. My work suffered, and other reporters finished the Deep Tunnel series. I became increasingly jumpy.

One afternoon, Harry called me in to his office and motioned me to a chair.

"Meg, how are you doing?" The softness in his eyes reflected genuine concern.

I broke down, sobbing. "Harry, I don't know what to do. I can't seem to think of anything else except poor Alfreda dying…the bomb…"

Harry looked discomfited. "Why don't you take some time off? Maybe get out of the city for a while, clear your thoughts," he suggested.

I thought of the little cottage my grandparents left me. That weekend, I packed up Minerva and moved to Bramble. I told myself it was only for a week or two. Months passed. Harry didn't press me, but one day I told him I wasn't coming back to Chicago. He offered me the "Miss Polly's Opinion" post. I hesitated at first. After all, an advice columnist is a long way from investigative reporting. But in the end, I accepted the job, and found to my surprise that I actually enjoyed being Miss Polly.

§

What was I going to tell Harry tomorrow? I carried my plate and glass to the kitchen and sat down at the table. I looked over my notes and thought about murder. Means, motive, opportunity. I grabbed my notepad and pencil and began jotting down questions and ideas. I had made my decision.

Chapter 8

Only in detective fiction do reporters do nothing except investigate and track down leads. Much as I wanted to wade into probing the murder of Simon Porter, I couldn't avoid the stream of everyday life. I pulled into a parking spot in front of the Bushel O'Bargains—an affectation of the first order, its prices comparable to Gold Coast food shoppes. Attracting a major food chain was one of the few benefits promised by the Porter-Burton plan that appealed to me. I went inside.

Clutching my grocery bag containing tiny cans of gourmet cat food, a treat for Minerva and priced just a few dollars less than the Pentagon's annual budget, I emerged from the store's frigid air-conditioning into the scorching afternoon. I put the bag in the car and prepared to drive home. Down the street, a slab-sided black Lincoln glided up to the curb. Edwin Porter and Travis Burton emerged from the vehicle and mounted the steps of the Memory Meadows Funeral Home. An attractive woman was with them, probably Simon Porter's widow, Susanne. The fourth person was Brad Trinder.

After the group was inside, I walked over to the mortuary, and stood on the sidewalk, pondering my next move. I had no intention of chatting them up, as I deplore the intrusion of the media on people in grief or pain. The group was probably making arrangements with Winn Jacobson, the funeral director, for Simon Porter's body.

I'm not proud of my next actions. I ascended the stairs to the small porch and peered through the door's oval window. I couldn't recall ever attending a morning visitation, so I was confident that a receptionist or greeter wouldn't be on duty. I pulled open the door and slipped inside.

Memory Meadows was originally a private residence. Victorian in design, the interior had been converted to its present use with little change. The walls were painted a soothing pale green. Lighting sconces, originally fueled by lamp oil, lined the hallway, the floors of which were covered in lush dark carpeting. A massive walnut staircase curved up to Jacobson's office and private living quarters on the second floor. The chilled air was oppressive with the cloying scent of carnations and gladioli.

Thick dark-green velvet draperies served as floor-to-ceiling doors to the two rooms opening off the entry hall. I glanced into the parlor on the right. To my relief, no coffin containing someone's Aunt Maudie rested on the raised faux-marble viewing pedestal. The drapes were drawn across the doorway to the room on the left, where I could hear voices in conversation. Having come this far, I abandoned any remaining semblance of propriety and squinted through the small opening in the curtain where it met the doorframe.

Winn Jacobson, unctuous as ever, intoned, "Please be seated." He motioned the group to a brocaded love seat and matching chairs. Turning to Edwin Porter, he asked, "Will this be comfortable?"

Burton replied, "Fine, fine. I appreciate not having to climb those stairs to your office." Today, the old gentleman was more casually dressed than at the town meeting. Like many older people, he must feel chilled even in the unseasonal September heat, for he wore a light sweater under his sport coat. Gripping his cane, he shuffled slowly to one of the chairs. The others seated themselves. Trinder remained standing to the right of the settee, just out of my sight.

"Such a sad and difficult time." Jacobson warmed to his subject, "Be assured we will serve you and your departed loved one with grace and dignity…"

Susanne Porter interrupted. "Please, Mr. Jacobson, I'd just like to, well, to get this over with."

"Of course you do," said Jacobson, reaching out to pat her hand with one of his plump, white ones.

Porter, his faded blue eyes glistening with unshed tears, looked up at him. "My son Simon…before his time…" Wheezing, his voice trailed off.

The Widow Porter dabbed at her eyes with a tiny hanky she held in her ring-encrusted fingers. "I didn't mean that as harshly as it sounded…" Dab, dab. I noticed no tears either in her eyes or coursing down her exquisite make-up. She appeared to be in her thirties. She wore a tasteful dark suit, probably tailor-made to minimize her plumpish figure. Four-inch Ferragamo heels. Her dark hair was carefully arranged to look casual.

From my years living in Chicago, I knew this effect was not easily or cheaply achieved.

Travis Burton patted her knee as Jacobson purred, "There, there. We at Memory Meadows understand your grief." He turned away from Susanne Porter and started toward where I was. Quickly, I moved away from my hiding place behind the draperies and flattened myself against the wall. My heart pounded.

"As you know," Jacobson continued, "we've already arranged with one of our sister chapels in Chicago to care for your husband after the, um, remains are released."

A rustling sound, then Jacobson's voice continued, "Here you are, Mrs. Porter. Here's a brochure, which should help you. Bramble doesn't have a very large Jewish population, so we don't keep any simple caskets in our selection room. However, you can choose a simple casket in keeping with your faith from the ones shown in this brochure, and we'll handle the details…"

"Oh," said Susanne. "I'm not sure…"

Edwin Porter said, "I'm afraid there's nothing any of us can do about the mutilation of my son's body in the autopsy, or with the delay in his burial, but we can certainly make sure that as much as possible of our care for the dead is followed. If you don't mind, Susanne…"

"Oh, thank you," Susanne said. "I'm really at a loss."

I sidled back to the gap in the drapes and peeked in again.

"We will be pleased to assist in any way we can, Mr. Burton," responded Jacobson.

Discussion continued about costs, transportation, and the like. The group gathered up their belongings. I panicked. I couldn't get caught lurking in the draperies of the funeral home like something from a B-rated horror film. Careful not to let the front door bang behind me, I fled the realm of eternal rest.

§

Once outside, I thought back to the scene at Memory Meadows. People deal with grief differently, but something was amiss with those people. Tension, coldness. On my way back to my car, I paused. I had to find out what Brad Trinder was doing with Travis Burton and the Porters. In front of Johnny's Bait Emporium, I pretended fascination with the display of lures and other fishing paraphernalia in the flyblown window until, out of the corner of my eye, I saw the group emerge from the funeral parlor. I ambled back and intercepted them as they prepared to climb into their car.

Trinder looked uncomfortable. "Why, hello again, Meg." He caught my curious stare and glanced away. "We were making arrangements for Mr. Porter's remains. His interment will be in Chicago later this year after…after all this…" He stopped, looked uncertain how to proceed.

I wouldn't let him off that easily. "I didn't know you knew Simon Porter," I said pointedly.

Trinder ran his finger inside his collar as he stepped around the car to the driver's side. "I guess it didn't come up the other day. I'm employed by Porter-Burton Enterprises."

I stared vacuously as he drove off.

So Brad Trinder works for PBE. Why hadn't he said so when we heard the news about Simon Burton being killed?

We had only rudimentary facilities for processing crime-scene evidence, so the coroner would hold Simon Porter's body until forensic reports came back from the lab in Chicago. They'd be in town for a while, so I'd see them again.

Chapter 9

Minerva circled around my ankles in welcome as I stepped inside my house. She watched as I tipped a can of the high-end cat food into a dish, and placed it and a bowl of fresh water on the floor. She sniffed the food and walked away. Fine.

I made a peanut butter and banana sandwich for myself, and sat down at the computer to enter my thoughts. A few minutes later, the phone rang. It was Sally.

"Hi, Meg. Craig and I decided on a date for our house-warming party. Honestly, between his schedule and mine..."

"Hang on. Let me get something to jot down the details. And what can I bring?"

"Don't bring a thing. Just you." She paused. "But I do want to ask a favor, Meg."

"Sure."

"We're having only a dozen or so guests, and I thought it would be nice to hand-deliver the invitations. I wonder if you could go with me. You know some of these people better than I do socially. Like Jake, who did most of our plumbing."

I wasn't sure why Sally thought I hob-nobbed with Jake (that chewing tobacco!) and his wife, Marlene—maybe because they lived a few houses down the road from me—but I consented to help out. This would be a great chance for me to talk about the murder with some of the Bramble residents.

Sally and I agreed to meet at my house the next evening, when most of the residents would be home. No one ever called ahead and made an appointment to visit neighbors in Bramble.

§

We started with "Cottage Row," since we could walk to them all. Actually, we could kayak to them, but the idea of Sally in her sundress, Sophia Loren sunglasses, and tasteful sandals…

The houses comprising "Cottage Row" were all on the lakefront, and several had short piers jutting into the water. Every family had a sailboat, canoe, or some other small craft docked or pulled up on shore. Each home had both the charm and the disadvantages of having started life as a vacation house. Or as one of my neighbors once commented, the improvements were made on weekends with a case of beer and a sledgehammer.

The lots were smallish, but with lots of trees. Like the rest of the town, we fought unending battles with the bramble or buckthorn. Louis and Jon would still be at their restaurant, so we started with the Fultons.

"Charming" is the word that best describes the Fultons' home: white clapboard siding, gray shutters at the windows, and a bright red front door. Mums burst forth in purples and golds from the window boxes under the windows. A ramp to the door had white railings on each side with pots of flowers clipped to them. As Sally and I walked up the ramp, Nina, deftly manipulating an aluminum walker, opened the door. "Sally. Meg. What a nice surprise! Come in, come in," she said as she ushered us into the tiny living room. "Sit, sit."

We sank into the couch. Covered with chintz, it was flanked by two end tables holding lamps with ruffled shades. Photographs of the Fultons' children and grandchildren covered the walls. Highly polished oak floors surrounded the blue and white hooked rug in the middle of the living room.

Nina placed her walker to one side of a chair across from us, and perched on its edge. Catching our glance, she said, "I use a wheelchair when I'm out and about with Ben, but it's cumbersome around the house."

"What is that divine aroma?" I asked.

"A batch of cookies. They should be ready soon, and you can sample them."

"We came to invite you to a party at my home," said Sally, as she handed an invitation to Nina. "The house is a long way from being exactly the way we want it, but we want to celebrate our progress."

"We've seen a lot of your workmen at the hardware store," replied Nina, adding with a twinkle, "Good for our business. The outside of your home is lovely. So glad someone like you and your husband bought it. It was becoming quite an eyesore. We would love to come."

"Well, well! What have we here?" Ben Fulton boomed a greeting as he came into the room. "How's that bathroom of yours, Meg?" Only in Bramble would someone open a conversation by asking for a bathroom update.

"Just fine, Ben. All finished," I answered.

Nina started as a buzzer sounded in the kitchen. "The cookies. I took advantage of the cooler weather today to make a batch of Ben's favorite chocolate chips." With some awkwardness, she rose to her feet and reached for her walker. As she went slowly toward the kitchen, she said over her shoulder, "You must stay and have some—and fresh lemonade."

"Great!" Sally and I replied in unison.

Ben patted his paunch and smiled. "Never have been able to say no to Nina's cooking."

The sound of dishes rattling came from the kitchen.

"I'd best go help," said Ben.

When he was out of earshot, I asked Sally, "What is Nina's condition? I've lived here a while now, but never heard what caused her disability."

"Some sort of accident. Part of the reason they moved back here when Big Ben died was it was easier to cope in a small town without much traffic. She sees a physical therapist every week in Walnut Creek. The Fultons close the hardware store every Thursday afternoon so Ben can drive her there."

We broke off our conversation as the Fultons came back. "Here we are," said Ben. He carried a heavy tray laden with goodies and an enormous pitcher of lemonade, waited for Nina to seat herself before setting the tray down on the coffee table.

Nina passed around the plate of cookies while Ben filled our glasses.

"Love your cookie plate," commented Sally. "Royal Doulton, isn't it?"

"Why, yes. We bought it shortly after we moved here. We've sold all but this one plate. The pattern's called 'Brambly Hedge.' So appropriate, we thought."

"Absolutely," replied Sally. "Did you also know…?"

The two women were soon in deep conversation about hallmarks, kilns, firings, and other related esoterica.

I placed my glass and plate carefully on linen doilies scattered about on the coffee table, and turned to Ben. "Terrible thing, the murder, isn't it?"

"Shocking," Ben replied. "We've never had anything like that here in Bramble. One of the big papers in Chicago once called us 'The Town That Crime Forgot.'"

I chuckled, thinking of our weekly rag, the *Bramble Buzz*. Its Police Blotter routinely carried items such as squabbles between neighbors about weeds having the nerve to grow over property lines. Last December, Bramble residents were amazed to see one of the *Buzz* reporters listed for suspicious behavior. She had been driving around town after dark, taking notes of the annual Christmas house decorations contest.

"I hear from Chief Koenig that you're doing a write-up for the *Journal-Times,*" said Ben, his face alive with curiosity.

"Yes. Just a few paragraphs." Inwardly, I groaned. Sally and Craig knew of my alter ego, Miss Polly, and my previous career as a reporter, but the rest of the town thought I did freelance writing. I had hoped to keep a low profile on my reporting so that villagers would be more open in talking about the murder.

"The Chief came by the store today," said Ben. "I guess he's checking on all of us who had a stake in the Porter-Burton deal. He wanted to know our whereabouts the night of the murder. Can't imagine that any of us would do such a thing." Ben leaned forward conspiratorially. "He said Simon Porter was shot."

"Really?" I knew this already from the coroner, but let Ben continue.

"Yep. We all thought Simon had been run over by accident." Ben paused. "He asked me about my guns. I have a shotgun and a deer rifle I use for hunting. Just like a lot of us here in Bramble."

Leaning forward, I asked, "What kind of weapon was used to kill Simon?"

"Chief Koenig didn't say exactly, but since he didn't want to see my guns, I'm thinking it must be a handgun."

"You don't have any handguns, then?"

"We carry them at the store, of course. But we don't have any around the house. What would I need one for in Bramble?" He laughed. "I'd probably end up shooting myself in the foot.

"In any case, Nina and I were here all evening like always. It gives you a funny feeling, though, being questioned like that. As if you're a suspect or a 'person of interest,' as they say on television."

"That must be scary," I said.

Ben nodded. "A lot of people in Bramble are angry and upset over the development plans.

I've known most of those people for years, watched some of them grow up here. After that meeting the other night..."

"What's your feeling about the development, Ben?" Sally asked. She and Nina had finished their rapturous discussion of china patterns.

"I think that the town will grow to the point that 'mom and pop' businesses like ours will be a thing of the past. Big-box stores will come in, undercut prices, and..." Ben shook his head. "I guess we'll retire earlier than we planned."

§

Dusk was descending, bathing the lake in soft lavenders and pinks. Sally and I stopped for a moment to enjoy the scene. Two wood ducks swam by, a string of ducklings trailing behind them. I tried not to think of how this idyll would be sacrificed to motorboats. Sally placed a hand on my arm.

"Do you think we should postpone giving out the invitations until tomorrow when it's not so dark?" Her eyes scanned my face.

"Gee, Sally, it's only eight-thirty."

"I know. It's with the murder and all..."

"I guess I hadn't thought about that." Even after being spooked the other night after the meeting, it had not entered my head that the murder of an out-of-town real-estate developer might have an effect on our safety. This was Bramble—not Chicago where two women walking alone down a dark, deserted street was never a good idea.

"I guess I'm rattled a bit," said Sally. Echoing my thoughts, she continued, "I shouldn't be, I know. This is Bramble, after all."

Glancing down Red Fox Lane, we saw several cars lined the road in front of the Winters' house and light shone from their windows.

"Looks like 'Pete's Posse' is rallying around," commented Sally.

"After all his threats about the development, he needs all the support he can muster."

"Do you think he did it?" Sally asked. "I don't know him. We have sewers in town, so we don't use his service."

"I've known Pete for as long as I've lived here. He's always been a hot head, but it's hard to imagine him actually killing someone." I thought back to his words after the town meeting. Some-one did do a lot more than protest. Was it Pete?

"I agree with him that we must fight the development of the lake shore," said Sally. "But I'm glad it's too late to stop in. I really don't want to get into some heated discussion right now with Pete and his buddies."

I would've liked nothing better than to talk with Pete and his friends right now, but said instead, "You're right, Sally. Might be awkward to deliver a party invitation right now, in any case."

We turned back to my house. Sally declined my offer to come in for a cup of coffee, and drove off.

§

Next day, after Sally opened the library and turned it over to her assistant, we started off. Pete Winters would be out working, and his wife, Kim, worked irregular hours at the hospital, so we started with the Tigrans.

As we arrived, we saw Marlene Tigran out back wrestling with two bed sheets. I had no idea anyone dried their laundry outdoors any more.

We walked over to her.

"Hi, Marlene!"

"Be with you in a minute," she mumbled, her mouth holding two or three clothespins.

Carrying the dry laundry, Marlene led the way into her house from the back door. "Watch your step!"

Clothes and toys were strewn across the small entrance, which doubled as a utility room. Only the wall to the left of the door was empty, save for an automatic washer. I sensed Sally the Neatnik tense at the disarray.

Marlene's eyes and nose were red, as if she'd been crying. "Jake promised he'd drive his pickup to Sears and get a gas dryer. That was two weeks ago. We ordered it. It's in. But…"

Like the cobbler whose children have no shoes, I thought. Aloud, I said, "Well, he's a busy guy. Did a wonderful job on my bathroom." Good grief, I'm going on about bathrooms, too.

"Don't even start me about our bathroom," Marlene said, brushing back a sweaty strand of fiery red hair. Marlene was an attractive woman in her thirties. She had beautiful blue, almost violet, eyes, and her figure was holding its own against the effects of time, gravity, and three children. I could hear the kids giggling in the living room as they presumably watched television. I could also hear the sofa complaining with the unmistakable sounds of children bouncing on it.

"The kids don't have classes today," Marlene said. "School's hardly started, and already the teachers have to go to some 'institute,' whatever that is. Both today and tomorrow."

Moving to the kitchen, the three of us perched on stools around an island counter. Daisies past their prime drooped from a vase in the middle. Children's artwork adorned the refrigerator door. I often wonder what future archaeologists digging through our modern-day ruins would make of doors with all manner of messages held in place with magnets. Several tattered romance novels were on a shelf near the sink.

"All I have in the house right now is Kool-Aid," said Marlene.

"Oh, please don't bother," replied Sally, as she proffered a party invitation to Marlene.

Marlene's hands shook and her eyes grew moist as she read it.

"Why, why…that's so nice. We hardly ever get invited to things like this. The kids…"

"Craig and I hope you and Jake can come. He's done such a great job on the house." Seeing Marlene's face fall, Sally hurried on, "Not just as a thank you. We'd like to get to know you two better."

Marlene brightened. "I'll check with Jake when he gets home—he's finishing up a job—but I know we'd both love to come."

Sally made as if to leave. I quickly began my line about the murder, "It's a terrible thing about—"

"The murder," Marlene finished. "Awful. Awful. Jake was so excited about the possibility of more work if the development happened. Do you suppose they'll continue with the plans?"

"Well," said Sally, "they have quite a bit of money invested already. Legal fees, permits, and such."

"Chief Koenig came by yesterday and wanted to know where we were the night Simon was killed. Like, where could I be? Get a baby sitter so I can go kill someone?"

"Did Koenig talk with Jake, too?" I asked.

"Yeah, I guess so. I was putting the kids to bed when Koenig was here, so I'm not sure what was said. Anyway, Jake was here the night of the murder."

From the living room came the shrill voices of the kids arguing. We said hasty good-byes and retreated through the back door.

Chapter 10

As I poured cereal and milk into a bowl the next morning, the radio crackled with the weatherman's cheery news of continued heat and humidity. No report from the Chicago CBS affiliate about Bramble's murder, but that wasn't surprising; we're a long way from the city. I finished breakfast, showered, dressed, and went downstairs to wait for Sally.

§

As we passed their house, the Fultons waved to us. Ben Fulton was assisting Nina into their customized handicapped van, as they left to open their hardware store for the day. Next door, Jake's plumbing truck was already gone, but the Tigran children, who seemed to be dressed only in pajamas, were chasing one another in a game that involved a garden hose and an ever-growing puddle of mud. Marlene would be hanging out wash again today.

We moved by the next empty cottage, its pitted blacktop driveway already shimmering a message of another hot day ahead. Rumor had it that the vacant properties in Cottage Row were in foreclosure. Having empty houses standing bleakly on the lake shore was not only depressing, but also increased the likelihood they would fall to the developers.

No one was home at the Winters' house. As we reached the door of the Banicki house, Sally said, "I love this old manual doorbell." Mounted on the middle of the door, the solid brass device was ornate, its dull patina showed its age. As Sally twisted the turn on the outside, the bell on the other side of the door rung.

Tony Banicki opened the door and peered over his half-round eyeglasses. His expression resembled a constipated prune. A glimmer of recognition crossed his face. After all, I waved to him almost every morning as he paddled by in his old wooden rowboat. "Oh, Miss Smyth..." His face relaxed slightly.

"Hi, Tony," I chirped. As a rule, I don't chirp much, but somehow it seemed the thing to do to counteract Tony's severe countenance. "This is my friend, Sally Montrose."

"I believe we've met. You're a librarian in town."

"Yes. We stock all of your textbooks." Anatole (Tony) Banicki was a professor of European studies at Woodrow Wilson College in Walnut Creek. "May we come in?"

Tony sighed, held the door wider, and motioned us inside.

Sally asked, "Do you mind if I look at the back of your lovely door bell?"

"If you wish." He moved aside so we could view the inside of the door.

"How does it work?" I asked.

Tony defrosted a bit as he launched into a long and complicated description of the bell's innards. Sally listened intently while I studied Tony. In his mid-fifties, Tony was tall, but stoop-shouldered. He had lost all of his hair, except for a longish gray fringe over his ears and around the back of his head. With half-glasses perched on his nose, he resembled a reedy Ben Franklin.

Concluding his lecture on the doorbell, he led the way into the living room. Seated by the fireplace was a wizened woman, covered with a crocheted blanket. She fixed a rheumy-eyed stare on us. Tony walked over to her. "*Matka,* these two women have come to visit us."

"How do you do, Mrs. Banicki," I said, gently taking one of her hands in my own. "I'm

Meg Smyth, and this is Sally Montrose." Sally smiled and nodded.

"Gita. My name is Gita." A smile flickered across her face. "Mrs. Banicki was my mother-in-law." The smile vanished. "Late mother-in-law. Gone now. Everyone's gone. Cold. It's always cold. Here, there..." The elderly woman withdrew her hand from mine and plucked fretfully at her blanket.

Tony tucked the wrap more snugly around his mother, and gestured for us to sit down. As he seated himself on the worn sofa next to us, green and yellow argyle socks peeked out incongruously from his scuffed leather slippers. I noticed his face soften as he assisted her. I bet she knitted the argyle socks, and he was kind enough to wear them.

"We were about to have some tea. Would you like some?" Tony asked us, reluctance in his voice.

"That would be lovely," said Sally. "Wouldn't it, Meg?"

"I'll be right back," said Tony.

We gazed around us. The furniture was old and close to threadbare in places, but meticulously clean. A lovely floral rug, now faded to a dusty rose, covered the wood floors. Ashes in the fireplace attested to attempts to counteract Mrs. Banicki's chill. On the mantel was a clock in a walnut case, its brass winding key next to it. In the place of honor was a photograph of Tony with some other young men. I walked over to it and saw that the group held sculls. A college rowing team, judging by their ages. Tony was in the back row, handsome and grinning. Unlike in the Fulton home, there were no other photographs or personal items displayed.

"Are you Tony's friends?" asked Gita Banicki.

"We both live here in Bramble," I said, avoiding a direct reply. "In fact, I'm a few houses down. The Rasmussens' place."

"Tony?" her voice quavered.

"He'll be right back. He's getting tea ready."

Tony returned, carrying a tray with mugs of tea and a box of butter cookies. The room was quiet except for the ticking of the clock. Sally put down her food, walked over to Gita and said, "My husband and I are giving an open house, and we'd love to have you and your son come." She handed Gita an invitation.

Gita turned the invitation over and over, as if it were a prized possession. She looked up at her son. "Wouldn't that be lovely, Tony?"

I could tell Tony was less than thrilled, but to his credit, he replied, "We'll try to attend. It depends on how Mother is, of course. Thank you for asking us."

"Terrible news about Simon Porter," I ventured.

"Who?" asked Gita.

I could've kicked myself. I shouldn't have assumed she knew about Porter's murder. Now I had the unhappy task of telling her about it. I kept the details to a minimum, and tried to reassure her that she had nothing to fear. As I talked, she twisted the invitation back and forth in her hands until it was nearly in shreds.

"So much evil in the world," commented Gita. "I thought it would be different here. Violence. Cop..." She mumbled something unintelligible. I strained to hear.

Tony said, "Yes, Mother. We'll watch television later."

"No cop…"

"No, no cops and robbers." He gave a short laugh that sounded rusty from disuse. "*Matka,* that's Polish for Mother, becomes terribly upset during the violent programs on TV. I try to stay away from them, but it's hard to do these days."

"We'd best be going," I said. Sally and I rose to leave.

"I'm so pleased to have met you," I murmured, pressing Gita's arm. It was then I noticed the numbers faintly tattooed there.

Gita pulled away and looked at me in confusion. Her eyes closed and her head drooped forward until her chin rested on her chest. Her son rearranged the covers around her once more.

§

As Sally and I set off down the walk, I said, "I feel awful. That nice old lady. I had no idea she didn't know about the murder…"

"Was that a concentration camp identification mark on her arm?" Sally asked.

"I'm pretty sure it was. My friend and neighbor, Alfreda, in Chicago, had one, and it looked similar."

"That explains why there weren't more family photos," Sally said.

"Yes. Tony is all she has."

Chapter 11

I glanced toward Pete Winters' house. His truck still wasn't there. Max Trent was next on our list, but at this time of day, he would be busy at the Liberty Café, so I suggested to Sally that we go there for lunch. We could chat with him after the noontime rush was over.

She gave me a look that made me think I might have toadstools sprouting from my ears. "Eat? At the Liberty Café? At the truck stop?"

"Cheer up," I replied. "You can have a Belly Buster Burger."

§

As we pulled in between two eighteen-wheelers, Sally gazed about her. Neil Armstrong couldn't have been more amazed at sights he encountered on his lunar stroll.

"People actually eat here? I mean, not just truckers?"

I locked the car and followed her eyes to the handful of passenger cars scattered about the lot. I decided not to reveal that from time to time, blissfully ignoring the possibility of clogged arteries, I came here for an occasional burger and beer.

As we crunched across the gravel toward the restaurant, we both noticed the fuchsia neon sign urging us to EAT. Except the "A" was dead. *E T.* We looked at each other.

"Extra-Terrestrials?" she asked.

"Et. Past perfect of eat. Eat, ate, had et."

Sally guffawed. Yes, guffawed. Beneath her perfectly groomed exterior beats the wicked heart of a fellow grammarian. Barely gaining control of ourselves, we entered the building.

Racks with free publications listing used cars and summer rentals were just inside the door. We paused at a display table filled with key chains, pine-shaped cardboard air fresheners, candy, chewing gum, and toothbrushes.

Sally lifted an eyebrow. "Toothbrushes?"

"There are a few cabins in the back for long-haul truckers. Not the kind of hotel where you can call down to room service if you forget something essential."

A waitress behind the counter called over, "You here to eat?"

That set us off again. "Yes," we gasped through repressed giggles.

The waitress grabbed two greasy menus and, her short skirt swaying as she sashayed ahead of us, led us over to a booth. She took a swipe at the table with a rag that last saw action bandaging the head of a Revolutionary fife player, handed us our menus, and left us to contemplate the selections. Returning in a few minutes with two scratched plastic glasses of water, she took a notepad and pencil from her pocket.

"What'll it be?"

"Belly Busters with everything," I said.

"Fries with that?"

"Sure. And a couple of Diet Cokes."

She grabbed our menus and sauntered away.

Sally stared at me. "I didn't want—"

"Sally, you must work on broadening your horizons."

"It's not my horizons I'll be broadening."

"That's why we're having Diet Cokes."

§

We tucked into our burgers. Okay, tucked is a bit of a stretch. I grabbed mine and wrapped my mouth around it, while Sally daintily pulled off the bun and ate what remained with a knife and fork.

Whilst we were chomping and nibbling, respectively, I noticed there were only a few patrons in the other booths. I glanced over to the lunch counter just as Max emerged from the kitchen. Seeing us, he waved and walked over.

"Hi, girls."

"Hi, Max," I replied. "You know my friend, Sally Montrose?"

He smiled at Sally. "You and your husband have been rehabbing that house in town. Howdy, Madam Librarian."

I didn't dare look at Sally. Being called "Madam Librarian" was one of her pet peeves. Max was probably safe as long as he didn't sing a few bars from *The Music Man.*

"Hello, Max." said Sally. "Busy day?"

"The usual lunch madhouse. Pretty much over now. Gives us time to get ready for the dinner crowd and restock our food supplies. Only one topic of conversation, of course—the murder."

"Anything new, Max?" I asked.

"Lots of theories. Chief Koenig was just in here, and said they're still looking for the gun."

"Really?" I leaned forward. "I would think it's long gone. Probably in the lake. It's only about a hundred yards from the construction yard."

"Yeah. He said the shells they found were from a nine-millimeter handgun."

Good grief. The Chief is not exactly the soul of discretion. Incompetent idiot.

"I'm sure we'll hear more pretty soon," said Sally. "The joys of a small town."

"Yep. I guess a lot of people won't miss Simon Porter much. Wonder if the development plans will still go through. I sure hope so."

Don't argue with him, Meg. I needn't have worried, as Sally took up the gauntlet.

"I heard you the other night at the meeting, Max," said Sally. "How much business do you think the development will bring in to your café?" She gestured at the interior, stopping when her eye caught those of a dusty buffalo head mounted on the wall to her right.

"Probably not so much for the café, although there will be more trucks bringing food and stuff for the additional shops in town," he replied. "The increased income will mostly affect our motel. We can finally enlarge it, put in a swimming pool…" He continued along these lines for several minutes.

Sally interrupted. "Speaking of our house, Max, I wonder if you and your wife would like to come to our open house." Sally reached in her purse, pulled out an invitation, and extended it to him.

He took the invitation with surprising delicacy, as if it were a piece of fine china. "I'm sure we'd like to come, but you'd best ask the wife."

The wife? Not *my* wife? Exercising Herculean restraint, I refrained from rolling my eyes.

Sally asked, "Is Claudie here? I'd love to talk with her."

"She's out back," Max replied, handing back the invitation. "She runs the motel."

"Great," I said. "We'll go over and chat with her."

§

As Sally and I twined through the stand of trees that separated the restaurant from the motel, I said, "I didn't know you knew Max's wife."

"Oh, yes. She's at the library quite a bit. She must have read every romance novel we have. Runs in the family."

"Huh?"

"Claudie's mother must've watched those old romantic movies. She named her daughter 'Claudette' after Claudette Colbert."

This time, I didn't forbear rolling my eyes.

The Interstate Sleepytime Motel, known in Bramble as the Royal Roach, consisted of six separate cabins. Judging by their size, a bed and shower were about all a guest could expect. Antennas perched on the cabin roofs. Although the paint on the wood siding needed refreshing, the buildings seemed to be in good condition. One even had some flowers dotting a small spot by the door.

We entered the office. Claudie Trent was bent behind the desk, a phone cradled between her shoulder and chin.

"Those linens were supposed to be delivered this morning! How can I run a motel and keep the health department off my neck if I don't have clean sheets and pillow cases?" She paused, listened to the response, then said, "They'd better be here within the hour!"

She hung up with more restraint than I expected. Catching my look, she said, "I've cracked two telephones already by slamming down the receiver. No point in that. Damn laundry service!"

Claudie walked over to us. Her anger seemed at odds with her appearance. She was a wisp of a woman. Brown came to mind, although she wasn't colorless, exactly. Her brown hair was limp, thinning, and dulled with gray. A hint of pink lipstick provided the only color to her face. Her hands reminded me of small birds with brittle bones.

"Hi, Sally. Hi, um…"

"Meg Smyth."

"Right. You live in the Rasmussens' cottage down the road from us."

"I inherited it from my grandparents." For some reason, houses in Bramble were known by the family who last owned them, not by the current residents.

Sally gave an invitation to Claudie. "My husband Craig, and I are having an open house. We finally finished the renovation of our downstairs. We'd love to have you and Max come. Max said we'd best clear the date with you."

"You mean, cater it?" Claudie asked.

Visions of Belly Busters served in Sally's formal dining room raced through my mind.

Sally replied, "Oh, no, no. As a guest." Sally was smooth. I detected no horror in her tone.

I turned away to hide my smile, and ambled across the small lobby to the bookshelves labeled, "Take One, Leave One." They provided no respite from my suppressed laughter, filled as they were with paperback romance novels, their lurid covers featuring bare-chested men with rippling muscles and bulging crotches. I picked up a book and thumbed through it. Marlene Tigran's name was scrawled on the flyleaf.

Claudie scanned the invitation, looked up, and said, "We'd love to attend." Turning to me, she added, "If you'd like to take that book along with you…"

"Oh, no, no," I said, replacing the book and hoping there was no horror in my voice.

"We'd better be going…" Sally began.

Claudie turned away from us and walked toward her desk.

"Have you heard anything new about Simon Porter's murder, Claudie?"

"No, it's pretty quiet here. I don't go over to the café, always bring something from home and eat here at my desk."

I would bet money that Claudie's luncheon choice elevated her a bit in Sally's estimation.

Undaunted, I pressed on, "How do you feel about the proposal for Prairie Lake, Claudie? I didn't see you at the town hall gathering."

"Max thinks the project would be wonderful. He's not the one trying to run the motel with no help."

"Surely, you'd be able to hire more…"

"Yeah. Right." Claudie's eyes narrowed as she looked around the small office. "Max is always talkin' the talk."

"Some things take time," Sally said. "I hope you and Max will be able to come to our get-together."

"Yeah. We'll try to make it. Thanks again."

§

As soon as we were away from the motel, Sally stopped and turned to me. "Okay, Meg, what are you up to?"

I put on my most innocent face. "What do you mean?"

"Don't give me that look. I know you too well. Why all the questions about the murder? You've brought it up everywhere we've been."

"Okay, you win." I sighed. "I told my editor I'd keep an eye out for any new information about the murder. A murder out here isn't big news in Chicago, but perhaps..."

"Oh, Meg. Be careful. People like Claudie look harmless, but so do small animals until they're cornered."

"Thanks for calming things down in there."

"I won't always be there to do that." Sally paused. "Unless..."

"Unless what?"

"Unless I help you dig around a bit."

"I don't know, Sally, if that's such a good idea."

"Sure it is. And besides, we can compare notes and make sure we haven't missed something." Her eyes danced with enthusiasm.

"What about Craig? What's he going to say about this?" I could feel myself weakening.

Sally was right. It would be good to have someone to compare theories and ideas with.

"Craig is so busy in what he calls his 'man cave,' that he's oblivious to the rest of the world." We laughed at the investment banker's idea of a man cave: no giant wide-screen television, no end-tables designed to look like golf tees, no snack bowls shaped like footballs—just an array of computers and telephones.

"Okay, let's try it," I said.

"Wonderful! Our first stop tomorrow: Gloria's Glamour." Sally said.

"What? The beauty shop?" I made a mental note to stop rolling my eyes so much; I'd wear them out.

"None other. There's no better place to pick up gossip. And," she added with a twinkle, "Chief Koenig's wife has a standing appointment for Saturday mornings. As do I." Sally eyed my shaggy coif. "I'll make an appointment for you too."

Chapter 12

My tresses weren't due for Gloria's artistry until early afternoon, so I decided to stop in at the Bramble Trust and Savings Bank beforehand. The bank held most, if not all, of the mortgages in town, so perhaps I could find out a bit about the houses in Cottage Row that were in foreclosure.

The bank reflected a time when financial institutions were sturdy buildings, their stolid massiveness exuding conservatism, reliability, and permanence. As I entered, the receptionist looked up from her desk just inside the door. "How can I help you?"

I asked for Mr. Trimble, and she directed me past a row of brass-caged tellers waiting to earn my trust and care for my savings. I crossed the marble floor to an enormous desk that could serve for signing international treaties. J. Forrest Trimble III, one of the bank's several vice presidents, stood and beamed at me. "Hello, Margrethe. What brings you to the bank on this fine day?" He motioned me to a seat facing the desk, and sat down.

As warm as the day already was, Trimble wore a three-piece suit and a white shirt stiff with starch. His head was nearly bald, and appeared covered with setae. I thought of the Chicago radio station that issues "comb-over alerts" on particularly windy days, and suppressed a chuckle.

"Hello, Mr. Trimble." Although he was about my age, being addressed by my full first name made me feel like a child about to ask a parent for an advance on her allowance. "I'd like to talk to you about mortgages."

His beam became radiant. "I'd be pleased to help you."

"I'm not in the market quite yet for a mortgage on my own house. My grandparents left it to me free and clear."

"Ah."

"I'm interested in the status of the other houses around me. Three of them are empty."

"Well, I can't share a lot of confidential information, of course," Trimble replied. "I can tell you that Bramble Bank owns the houses and the vacant lot at present."

"What about eminent domain?"

"Well…that's certainly a possibility." Trimble squirmed, and made minute adjustments to align the blotter on his desk. "We'll be posting legal notices in the *Bramble Buzz* about that."

"And Porter-Burton Enterprises? I thought they were set to snap up the vacant houses."

"They would like to, of course." Trimble gave me a wary look. "Negotiations are in progress. I can't say much more."

So PBE is interested, but hasn't bought them officially yet.

Trimble smiled. "Is there anything else I can help you with?"

"No, thank you. I was concerned about my neighborhood and the value of my house."

"I understand."

We shook hands, and I embarked across the marble expanse toward the door. And nearly bumped into Pete Winters, who was coming in.

"Hi, Pete."

"Oh, hello, Meg." He glanced toward Trimble's desk, and I followed his look. Another customer was just taking the chair I had vacated. "Guess I'll have to wait a bit." Pete walked over to a group of chairs to one side of the door. I joined him.

I trotted out my gambit. "Have you heard anything new about the murder, Pete?"

"Not much. They found a nine millimeter casing in the trailer at the old lumber yard."

I already knew this, so I waited, hoping Pete would continue. In my reporting days, I found that most people would say something just to fill the silence. I wasn't disappointed.

Pete went on, "Lot of people have nine-millimeter handguns. People like 'em for protection. Easy to shoot. Even a woman could use one."

"Do you own one?" I asked. To my relief, Pete didn't seem to think my question odd or out of place.

"Used to. A Glock pistol. Disappeared from my truck a while back."

I changed the subject. "Lots of people at the bank today."

"Yeah. I'm hoping to refinance my mortgage so I can hold on to my house. I don't want to lose it—or have PBE get it. I was in here last week starting the paperwork. That old guy, what's-his-name Porter, was here. So were Tony Banicki and his mother, and the two queers. Like old-home week." Pete caught my look. "Not that I'm against gays. Louis and Jon are okay, I guess, and they sure do know how to cook. Just uncomfortable around them, you know?"

Wanting to gather more information from Pete, I refrained—barely—from telling Pete off. I asked, "So who do you think shot Simon Porter?"

"Got no idea, Meg, but I'd like to thank the person who did." Catching my look, he added, "Not really, but he was a nasty piece of work." He sighed. "It won't make no difference. Porter-Burton won't pull out. They'll still ruin every-thing."

§

Leaving the bank, I walked toward Gloria's Glamour in the next block. I scuttled past The Clipper Snip, the barbershop where I usually had my hair cut, keeping my head down so I wouldn't catch the eye of Russ Banks, the owner. When I lived in Chicago and spent more and more time pursuing my career with the *Journal-Times,* I opted out of hair salons. I took to shorter hair and quick trips to a barber, habits I continued here in Bramble.

The pungent aroma of ammonia and hair-spray greeted me as I entered Gloria's Glamour

and gazed about the salon. I sat down in the waiting area, and picked up a movie magazine from
the table next to my chair. I flipped through pages
of vapid revelations about movie studs and star-
lets, referred to only by their first names, their
adoring fans needing nothing more to identify
them. I stifled a yawn.

"Meg?" Gloria bustled over to me. Short
and a bit pudgy, she had hair of a purplish shade
not found in nature, and permed in girlish ringlets.
This did not bode well. I stood up.

"That's me."

"Come right this way. Your friend, Sally,
is already here."

I waved to Sally, who, towel wrapped
around her head, was walking over to her stylist's
chair. I followed Gloria to a row of sinks, where a
young woman, holding a vinyl smock out to me,
stood waiting. "Hi. I'm Babsy Wilcox. I'll be your
shampoo girl today."

Just in time, I remembered my resolution
to cut back on rolling my eyes. What kind of parents would name their child Babsy? I donned the
smock, sat in the chair with my back to the sink,

and relinquished myself to the joy of having someone else wash my hair and massage my scalp.

Gloria beckoned me to her station. After she cranked my revolving chair higher, she looked at me in the mirror and said, "What did you have in mind?"

Swept along in Sally's enthusiasm the other day, I hadn't given a thought to what I wanted done with my hair. "Um…"

"How 'bout something like this?" Gloria whipped out a salon magazine and showed me a photo of an androgynous model with platinum hair and one eye. Well, she/he probably had two eyes, but a long glop of hair obscured her left one.

"Um…maybe not so radical?"

"Um," responded Gloria. This was developing into quite a stimulating conversation.

She turned a gimlet eye on my hair. "Okay," she said at last. "No asymmetrical cut. But not the same color you have now, right?" Gloria's contemptuous tone reduced my favorite drugstore color, Honey Lustre, to Baby Poo Brown. She handed me a sheet of paper with swatches of plastic hair glued to it. Powerless in the face of her bullying, I pointed to what I hoped would turn out to be a conservative light brown.

Only on a treadmill does time pass more slowly than in a beauty shop. Surrounded by the drone of inane conversations while my color processed, I began to doze off. A voice from a few chairs away penetrated my languor. "They'll never get eminent domain through the village board."

"I don't even know what eminent domain is," said another woman.

A discussion of eminent domain in a beauty salon? Who woulda thunk it? I looked around and listened as Frieda Koenig, the mayor's wife, explained, in some detail, eminent domain—the right of the government to seize land for public good, or even for economic reasons. Frieda Koenig held a law degree and served *pro bono* as Bramble's village attorney. She was talking to her sister-in-law, Gladys Koenig, our police chief's wife.

"But why does Fred think his board can't do it?" asked Gladys.

"Oh, they can, but it will take months, maybe years. So many hearings, paper work, legalities. I can't imagine that PBE wants to wait that long," Frieda said, lowering her voice a decibel or two. Her voice was still audible to most of the clients, even over the hum of dryers and chatter. Telling someone something in confidence in a beauty shop was impossible on so many levels. "Between you and me, eminent domain is a dead issue."

That explained Trimble's hemming and hawing. I made a mental note to check the *Buzz* for legal notices.

Gladys changed the subject. "My Billy says they've got a suspect," she said.

"Who?" asked Frieda.

"You know, that…"

"Time to wash out the solution," Babsy said in my ear. I jumped. She must've crept up behind me. She led the way to her bowl. I walked as slowly as I could, and all but flapped my ears to hear more of the Koenig women's conversation, but to no avail. Babsy sluiced water over my head once again.

Gloria seated me in her chair with my back to the mirror "so as not to spoil the surprise." I endured several eternities of clipping, teasing, and blow-drying. Finally, Gloria turned the chair so I faced the mirror to admire my new look.

"This is so *you!*" Gloria exclaimed. "A combination of waif and sophistication." I sat stunned. Staring back at me in the mirror was Andy Warhol.

"And," she burbled on, "We have a marvelous fiber product for you to take home to keep that look." Keep this look? And what in the world was a fiber product? All I could think of was whole grain bread and Special K cereal.

Hoping there was no discernable difference between a grimace and a grin, I gave Gloria a toothy smile, and resolved to dash home and wash my hair. Again.

The cashier handed me a tiny pink plastic bag containing a tube of the fiber stuff. She also gave me a cutesy pink bill for my afternoon at the shop. I stifled a gasp. Maybe I should've talked to Trimble about a mortgage, after all.

Sally finished up right after me and we left the shop together. Sally, of course, looked her wonderful self. She looked at my hair and bit her lip. Tears of mirth formed in her eyes. I tried to maintain my dignity, but soon we were clutching each other, laughing and snorting.

§

"Let's go have a drink at the hotel," suggested Sally. "I can't wait to discuss what I heard in the beauty shop. Besides, I feel all dressed up with no place to go."

I didn't share her sentiment, since I had a place to go—under my shower at home. But I was curious about what she found out. "A drink sounds wonderful," I replied. With luck, I'd see no one I knew.

We crossed the street and entered the Prairie Palace Hotel. The Palace was a three-story reddish-brick building, constructed in the early years of the Twentieth Century. The hotel's original mullioned, leaded-glass windows were still in place. Its accommodations, while not plush, were clean and tasteful, bearing little resemblance to the Trents' Interstate Sleepytime Motel. The Palace was small, having only twenty rooms. Its immense bar of wood, darkened by age, dominated the main floor. Dozens of bottles of liqueurs were backlit behind the bar and provided splashes of color. A few tables and booths filled the remainder of the space. Although the hotel had no restaurant, Happy Hour every afternoon, except Sunday, was a Bramble gastronomic event. The Heron Restaurant catered the food, and Sammy, the hotel's bartender for decades, served drinks of amazing potency.

We stood for a few moments as our eyes became accustomed to the dim lighting. "Oh, look!" said Sally, pointing to the bar. "Craig's here."

Craig Montrose, tall and slim, wore a lightweight sport coat over an open-necked shirt. He and Sally made a handsome couple, and still seemed in love with each other. I'm sure that's why Sally kept trying to "fix me up" with eligible men: so I could enjoy marital bliss, too.

We smiled and waved to Craig. My smile evaporated. He wasn't alone. On the barstool next to him was Brad Trinder. Sally and I walked over to them. Sally's news would have to wait.

Both men stood up. Craig said, "Hi, honey," and gave Sally a peck on the cheek. "I walked over from home. Thought I'd have a drink, then come by and meet you at Gloria's. Maybe entice you to have dinner with me." He waggled his eyebrows.

"We finished up a bit early at the salon," Sally replied. She turned to Brad and said, "Hello. I'm Sally Montrose."

"Brad Trinder," he replied, shaking her hand.

"And hello again, Meg," he said to me. "I see you have a new look. Very jaunty."

"Thank you," I said, writhing inside. Jaunty, indeed.

The men picked up their drinks, and the four of us moved to one of the empty booths. The Montroses sat on one side, Craig with his arm draped lightly around Sally's shoulders. Brad slid in next to me. I breathed in his smell. Clean. Soap, not cologne or aftershave. I became aware of the warmth of his body next to mine.

Sammy came over and took our drink order, and left plates of prawns and a selection of dipping sauces.

"Come to this bar often?" Brad grinned. I noticed he wore no wedding ring.

I laughed at the ancient pick-up line. "I should ask you that question, since you're a stranger in these here parts."

"The Porters, Travis Burton, and I are staying here in the hotel. When I came downstairs a few minutes ago, who should I see but Craig? I met Craig at an investment convention last year."

"Oh, are you in the investment field, too? Is that what you do for PBE?"

Before he could answer, Sammy came over with our drinks. The conversation moved on to the restoration project at the Montrose house, culminating in Sally inviting Brad to their open house.

"Will you still be in town next week?" she asked.

"I'm pretty much here until things are settled with the development. I rent a condo in the city, so I use it when I need to be in Chicago," he replied. "So count me in for your bash!"

To her credit, Sally didn't cringe. Her "bash" was certain to be a refined affair of tea-cakes and watercress finger sandwiches.

We chatted a bit more over our drinks until Craig said, "Sally, I made reservations at the Heron for us tonight. We'd best be on our way." He turned to Brad and me. "I'm sure Jon and Louis can add you both to our table."

We both declined to join them, and Craig and Sally set off for the restaurant, which was in the next block. "I'll walk you to your car," said Brad.

There was no way I could refuse, even if I wanted to—which I didn't.

As we reached the small parking lot next to Gloria's Glamour, he said, "I'd like to see you again, Meg." His brown eyes searched mine. "How 'bout spending a day in the city? Just bum around, nothing fancy. I need to do some things there this week."

"I'd like that." I told myself it would be a good chance to meet with my editor and go over some Miss Polly articles for inclusion in my next book. I could also drop off the film of the photos I took at the crime scene.

"Would Monday work for you?" he asked. "We could take the early morning train to the Loop together."

"Great," I said. "See you at the station."

What was I thinking? I have no idea who Brad Trinder is, where he's from, or most important, his connection with the land developers— and Simon Porter's murder.

Chapter 13

As I drove home, I opened my car windows. The oppressive heat of the day was cooling. Fall was in the air.

Minerva eyed me as I scraped the food from her bowl into the garbage, and put the bowl in the dishwasher. I opened the cabinet and took down the box of brown cardboard bits that passes for cat food and poured some into a bowl. Minerva responded by cleaning her rear end.

All I'd had since breakfast was an energy bar at Gloria's and a few nibblies at the Prairie Palace, so I zapped a frozen dinner in the microwave. I was restless after eating, so I decided to change clothes and take the kayak out for a bit. It was dusk, my favorite time of day for being on the water, as the colors melted into the softness of evening.

The boat glided along in contrast to my thoughts, which frothed and churned. Brad Trinder. Someone about to be arrested. Reporting. Pistols. Suspects. I turned for home, where I climbed into bed, too exhausted even for the shower I'd promised myself.

§

Sunday morning. I opened a groggy eye and squinted at the clock. It was almost noon. No church for me today. The phone rang. I made a grab for it, missed. Another grab. The cord had spiraled into a tangle, and was now only three inches long.

"Hello," I croaked.

"Hi, Meg!" came a cheery voice over the line. I groaned. Only one person I knew was this joyous at such an early hour.

"Hi, Sally."

"I didn't wake you, did I? You sound terrible."

"I always sound like this at the crack of dawn."

"The *crank* of dawn, you mean." She laughed alone at her little pun. "It's noon, Meg."

"Urg."

"I think we should put our heads together and go over what we found out on our visits and at the beauty shop. I'm dying to tell you what I heard."

"Urg."

"How soon can you come over here?"

"Some Thursday in the next millennium would be good."

"Ha ha." Forced laughter.

"Okay, okay." I knew she wouldn't give up. Like a dog with a bone. "Give me some time to put myself together."

"About two at my house?" Sally asked.

"Urg."

I staggered downstairs to the kitchen, started the coffee, and shook some more cardboard pellets into the cat dish. Miracle of miracles: the newspaper was on the porch today. I took it, a cup of coffee, and a tired donut from two days before into the living room, where I collapsed on the couch. My thoughts began to whirl again, but at a much slower speed than the night before.

I stepped into the shower and let the hot water stream over me. Before the water could turn cold, I emerged, toweled off, and braved the mirror. My hair wasn't too bad, I told myself. It'll grow.

§

Sally's and Craig's house is a lovely Victorian in the oldest part of Bramble, a block off Main Street. They had faithfully restored the outside.

Where it needed to be replaced, wood siding was cut to order and painted in shades of mauve, new replacement windows were custom-designed, slate roofing replaced layers of old asphalt shingles. It was again, after several years, a true "painted lady," with the millwork painted in authentic colors complementing the siding.

I walked up to the door, and rang the bell. The door was the original, in its center an oval glass etched with an intricate design.

Sally opened the door and gave me a hug.

In my best Julia Child voice, I asked, "Shall we retire to the parlor or to the music room?" Sally was a stickler for using historic terminology. No "living room" or "family room" in her Victorian house. No sir.

Sally grinned. "The parlor today, milady."

Sally took paper and pencil from an end table, while I retrieved my notepad from my bag.

"Down to business. What did you hear at Gloria's shop?" Sally asked.

"Great news. Frieda Koenig gave a mini-lecture on eminent domain to Billy's wife, Gladys. Frieda said the issue of eminent domain is about dead."

"Frieda should know. She's the village attorney."

"If so, the *Bramble Buzz* will carry legal notices about it."

"Wow! That is big news. Guess I'll have to move the next *Buzz* to the top of my reading list." Sally paused.

I continued, "Gladys confided that an arrest would be made soon in the murder."

"Who?" Sally asked.

"I don't know. The shampoo girl came up just then and shouted in my ear, so I missed it. What did you hear? You seemed so excited about it last night."

"Well, in my corner of the shop, I overheard Paula from the hotel say that there was hanky-panky going on there between Travis Burton and Susanne Porter."

"No one says, 'hanky-panky' any more, Sally."

"Okay, have it your way." With reluctant abandon, Sally rephrased. "Paula said Travis and Susanne were screwing their brains out."

Sally and I dissolved into laughter.

"That gives them both a motive to kill Simon Porter."

"We also know that Simon was killed in the trailer on the lot, and moved to the shovel of the backhoe, probably to make a statement," Sally said. "I don't think the perp's intent was to make it look like an accident."

"Perp?"

Sally nodded primly, and we laughed again.

"Moving on," I said, "there's the matter of the means. The casing the police found was from a nine-millimeter pistol. From what I've learned, it's an easy weapon to use—no special training needed, and a woman could fire it. Not much recoil, I guess. Pete said he had one, but it was stolen. We need to try to find out how many other people in Bramble own the same kind of gun."

"So we have to assume that everyone had the means to kill Simon."

"Or access to the means," I amended.

"'Means' also include the physical strength to move the body," said Sally. "Travis looks strong enough."

"Travis and Susanne have motive, of course. Travis isn't married. Wouldn't it be easier for Susanne to divorce her husband than to murder him?"

Sally thought for a minute, then said, "They're big-city society people, rich. Maybe there was a pre-nup between Simon and Susanne."

"I suppose everyone who's opposed to the development has a motive, depending on how strongly they feel about it. Pete Winters has been leading the charge, threatening PBE. Hauling those huge coils of plastic drainpipe around every day would make him strong enough. And he owned that gun, which may or may not have been taken from his truck."

Sally said, "The coroner said death occurred around nine or ten o'clock that night. Almost everyone in town had the opportunity to go over there and kill Simon in the trailer.

"The posing of the body narrows the field, I think."

"How so?"

"If the killer were someone who didn't care one way or another about the development, why bother arranging the body? And for that matter, who would care enough to shoot him in the first place?"

I referred to my notes. "The Fultons and the Tigrans were home with their spouses. In any event, Ben Fulton is not a young man and Nina is practically an invalid. Ben was adamant about not having a handgun in the house, but they do sell them at the hardware store. Jake Tigran is strong enough to move Simon's body, but he's in favor of the development. Marlene's on a pretty short leash, taking care of their kids."

"The Banickis." said Sally. "It's hard to imagine either of them involved in a murder. Tony is about retirement age, so he may be leaving the university soon, and Gita is well into her eighties and so frail. Tony may need to move his mother to an extended care facility in the near future. Perhaps in a warmer climate where the winters aren't so brutal."

"So if they planned to move anyway, selling to PBE would be a godsend, keep them from the hassle of viewings…"

"Viewings are wakes. You mean 'showings,'" Sally said.

"That reminds me. I happened to see Edwin and Susanne Booth, Travis Burton, and Brad Trinder the other day in Memory Meadows."

"What were you doing in the funeral home?"

Sally's expression alternated between shock and amusement as I related my snooping adventure. "What if you'd been caught? What would you have said?"

I had no answer. Sally shook her head.

"Susanne seemed to be in a hurry to settle the details with Winn Jacobson. I remember something else. She said she had arrived in Bramble that morning. If so, when did Paula see Travis Burton with her at the hotel?"

We pondered that for a moment. "Then there are Max and Claudie Trent," Sally said. "Max is all in favor of the development. Thinks his ship will come in. Claudie is a strange duck, and she sure doesn't share Max's enthusiasm for the lake plans. She's tiny, so moving a man's body even a short distance would be pretty much impossible."

"Unless Max helped her," I said. "But why kill Simon?"

Sally shrugged. "Still, working alone at the motel out there on the Interstate, Claudie may keep a gun in the office for protection."

"I suppose we should include Pastor Joe."

"Meg! That sweet man?" Sally was scandalized.

"Just to be thorough," I reassured her. "He's been careful to stay out of the construction controversy, but having more houses would bring in a few more souls to save."

"What about the Koenigs?" Sally asked.

"The mayor, the police chief, Frieda. Hmm. Means and opportunity, but motive?"

"I wonder if Frieda and Hizzoner have any stake in the development," Sally mused.

"What do you mean?"

"Well, maybe they own property in Bramble that would appreciate in value with the addition of the PBE homes. Or maybe Billy and Gladys Koenig do."

"That would be quite a conflict of interest. The mayor and his missus already are walking a thin line with her serving as village attorney," I said, "even if she isn't billing hours to the village."

"Bramble's version of nepotism," commented Sally.

I turned to my notes. "Are we missing anyone else?" I asked.

"The mystery man. Brad Trinder."

I felt my cheeks grow warm. "Right! What do we know about him? Did Craig mention anything when you got home last night?"

"We really don't know anything about Trinder," said Sally. "And as for Craig, the subject of Brad Trinder didn't come up last night."

"Ooh," I said.

"Don't go there," Sally warned, her face crimson.

"We haven't talked with Louis Briggs and Jon Dreher."

"They're in favor of the development."

"Louis is. He spoke out at the town meeting. We don't know how Jon feels about it," said Sally.

"True. Like the Trents, Louis and Jon may not agree on this."

"They're both young and in good shape. Like everyone else, they might have access to a gun. I can't get a handle on motive."

"Guess we need to have another meal at the Heron so we can chat with them," said Sally. "Tomorrow?"

"I have other plans."

"Oh?"

"Brad and I are spending the day together in the city."

Sally pressed her fingers to her temples, closed her eyes, and hissed, "Madam Sally knows all, tells all. I see hanky-panky in your future…"

Chapter 14

The phone was ringing as I entered my house. I set my purse down, and snatched up the receiver.

"Hello?"

"Hello, Meg dear. How are you? We hadn't heard from you about our visit…"

A spasm of anxiety shot through me. Visit? My parents moved to a retirement village in Arizona a few years ago. They stayed with me for a week or so last Christmas, and vowed never again to venture to the northern wilds of Bramble in winter. Meeting their plane at O'Hare, I concluded that denying the existence of cold weather must be a byproduct of the acclaimed "dry heat" of Arizona. Passengers from the Phoenix flight were dressed in summer shirts and slacks, and shivered their way down the concourse. When they returned to the Valley of the Sun, my parents left their "Michelin Man" down jackets, scarves, hats, boots, and mittens—all purchased in an emergency run to Eddie Bauer in Chicago—in my hall closet.

"Hi, Mom. How are you and Dad?" I began, hoping she'd give me a clue about their visit.

Did she tell me they were braving Christmas again in Bramble? Did I forget? Was I losing it?

"It's so good to hear your voice. It's been a while." Guilt, the gift that never stops giving.

"Well, I've been meaning to call you. Just busy…" Same lame excuse as always. I really should call them more often.

"We booked a flight for Thursday."

"Thursday? This Thursday?" I squeaked. I searched the table for something to write with, as she went on to give me the details.

"Why, of course, dear. That will give us time to unwind from our trip before the big event."

"Big event?"

"Meg, are you feeling okay? You sound…I don't know…odd."

"No, I'm fine, Mom."

"You're sure we won't be imposing? We're going right back on Sunday for the bunko tournament at the club. It was so sweet of Sally and Craig to invite us to their open house. Your dad and I can hardly wait to see what lovely things they've done to their home."

"Yes." I managed not to groan. "And it will be great to see you."

We made plans about where I'd pick them up at the airport.

"We love you."

"Love you too." I hung up the phone, and dialed Sally's number. She answered on the first ring.

"I will put a horse head inna bed wit' you. You are marked for death," I said.

Sally laughed. "You can't scare me, Meg. What's up?"

"My folks are coming to your open house!"

"That's wonderful!"

"Easy for you to say. The last time my mother was here, she alphabetized all the things in my pantry. Campbell's soup, Cats Delight litter, celery salt…

"Why didn't you tell me you'd invited them? Don't get me wrong. It's really nice of you and Craig to include them. But gee, some advance warning…"

"Well, I added them later."

"I thought you were only inviting a dozen or so guests," I said.

"The list grew somewhat. Your father was so helpful when Craig talked with him at Christmas time about the flooring. They spent hours in our basement discussing the pros and cons of hickory, oak, heart-of-pine. To be honest, I didn't expect your parents to come all this way for the party."

"And to see their darling daughter, don't forget," I said, chuckling. "Well, I must run along and start cleaning my house."

"Wait! What are you wearing for your date with Brad tomorrow?" I knew Sally's mouth was curved in her cat-that-ate-the-canary smile.

"I have no idea."

§

I trudged upstairs and pulled open my closet door. We'll just bum around, Brad said. Bumming around in Chicago is not quite the same as bumming around in Bramble. At least it would be "cooler near the Lake." Minerva eyed me from the bed. I scooped her up, put her down in the hallway, and closed the door. She whined and scratched at the door, but I didn't need the addition of cat hair, however well-intentioned, to my *ensemble*.

Deciding on slacks, blouse, a light jacket, and comfortable shoes, I headed down the stairs, stepping carefully over Minerva who, sprawled on a step midway down, ignored the gentle nudge I gave her with my foot. As I reached the bottom of the stairs, I glanced up and was rewarded by a baleful glare.

I fixed myself a grilled-cheese sandwich, opened a can of Coke, and took them both out to the dock. I slipped off my shoes, and dangled my feet into the cool water as I ate. Dark was closing in as I walked slowly back to my house. I looked over at the empty house next door as the dusk shadowed its windows. I felt chilled.

Chapter 15

Just a handful of trains stopped in Bramble each day on their way to Chicago. The early morning train left Bramble at 6:45 a.m. My dad referred to it as the Toonerville Trolley, but in reality, the train was part of the Amtrak rail system.

I left my car in the station's lot, walked over to a metal kiosk, and slipped a dollar into the slit bearing my parking spot number. There was not enough business to warrant a stationmaster, but the railroad hadn't abandoned parking as a source of revenue.

Not surprisingly, the Bramble train station was miniscule. It had no toilet facilities, vending machines, or coffee shop. It was well maintained, probably because it didn't see much use. Passengers bought tickets on the train from the conductor, or monthly passes from the terminal in downtown Chicago.

In one corner was a shelf with a few books that passengers could borrow, on the honor system, although most of the books were so dog-eared, that they weren't attractive enough for anyone to steal. Glancing at the titles, I saw among them a paperback, *Lusty Pirates.* I needed to see

Claudie at the motel again, so I reached for the book. I could use adding to her romance collection as a ruse.

Brad came up to me as I was tucking the book into my purse. "Hi, Meg." He eyed the book in my hand.

Flustered, I said, "I don't read these things. It's, er, for a friend."

Brad nodded and said nothing.

The bells on the crossing-gates outside began to ring. We went outside, stood on the platform and looked down the track. With a squealing and hissing of brakes, the train rolled to a stop. Its conductor swung down from the stairs, and stood waiting for the passengers—the two of us and three men in business suits, carrying briefcases— to board. Brad took my elbow and helped me up the steps. I was, of course, quite able to climb the two or three stairs, but I allowed myself to be assisted. I like to think of myself as Ms. Independent, but I'm always pleased by a gentleman's manners. And, after all, this was a date, wasn't it?

Brad pushed aside the doors into the car on the left, where we found seats together about halfway down. The train was already fairly full with passengers who had boarded in the towns on the route to Bramble. Most were commuters, reading or dozing at this hour, so the train car was fairly quiet.

Any worries I had about what we would find to talk about on the ride into the city quickly dissipated. Brad said he had been to Chicago a few times, but always on business. "I never left the hotel, except to go to dinner with a client," he said.

"I'm glad," I said.

He quirked an eyebrow at me. "How so?"

"I grew up in Chicago. When we had a day off school, we kids would hop on the bus and go to one of the museums or to the aquarium." Seeing his look, I hastened on. "They're not fusty old things with dioramas and dusty displays. The Museum of Science and Industry has a German submarine from World War Two that you can actually go through, a coal mine, and lots of interactive exhibits." I laughed. "Our mothers warned us that we were absolutely not to see the human development area, where they display fetuses in jars. So, of course, that's always where we went first.

We spent the rest of the ride talking companionably about music and movies. It was suddenly dark outside as the train entered the tunnel leading into the Ogilvie Center. Inside the train, the passengers began to gather their things and move down the aisle to the doors.

"I guess we're here," Brad said.

"That was a quick ride. Did you have anything specific you wanted to do today?"

"Let's get our business out of the way this morning, then meet somewhere and look around for the rest of the day."

"Sounds good."

We walked through the station and out into the busy streets toward a cabstand at the corner.

"Where are you headed?" I asked. "I'm headed over to Wacker Drive to the *Journal-Times* building. We could share a cab if you're going in that direction."

"No, I'm headed the other way." Brad looked at his watch. "Can we meet at your office around noon?"

"Okay. If I'm not in the lobby, ask for Harry Josten's office."

A cab pulled up. Brad opened the door for me. "See you at noon at the *Journal.*" He closed the door, tapped the roof of the taxi, and waited while the next cab in line drew up.

As I settled in and gave my driver directions, it dawned on me. I still didn't know what Brad was doing with Porter-Burton Enterprises

§

When I first went to work for the *Journal-Times,* I was fresh out of journalism school, having served an internship the summer before graduation. The newspaper business had moved from the days of Clark Kent and Jimmy Olson, linotype operators minding their lower case Ps and Qs, and reporters yelling, "Copy!" to some young apprentice standing by to take typewritten stories to an editor. Not one guy in a porkpie hat with a press card tucked in the band, a cigarette dangling from the corner of his mouth.

Typewriters were long gone, replaced on our desks by "dumb" computers linked to an enormous mainframe computer housed in a environmentally controlled room, which only a chosen few technicians were allowed to enter. The computer system went down several times during the course of the day, so we saved our work over and over—no simple task, since this was accomplished by shutting down our computer terminal, then booting it back up. A device similar to a traffic signal was bolted to one corner of the newsroom to warn us of an impending computer crash. When the light moved from green to yellow, the room was filled with cries of "Save, save!" as we all tried to save our work before the red light glowed with its terrible message.

Before I left my reporting job and moved to Bramble, CRT monitors atop large hard drives replaced the old mainframe and the traffic light was removed. In an odd mix of old and new, cubicles were installed around the battered old oak desks that once were butted up against each other.

As I walked through the newsroom on my way to Harry Josten's glassed-in office on its perimeter, it seemed quieter than I remembered, less exciting. The whiteboard was still in place with assignments and schedules scribbled on it. Did I miss it? To be honest, I did. But not enough to return.

§

Harry's door was open, so I tapped on its frame.

He looked up and a smile lit his face. "Meg! It's great to see you. Sit, sit. Just move that stuff." There were always piles of clippings, notes, and phone messages piled on every available surface. I once asked him how he found anything. "Cream will rise, Meg. Cream will rise."

Harry Josten was a fixture at the *Journal-Times*. He was smallish in build. His hair, carroty red when I first met him, was now gray and thinning. I noticed his fingers had ink on them, as usual—not from newsprint, but from using a fountain pen. He had a collection of inkwells and pens, and on his desk was a large green blotter pad instead of the usual calendar grid.

I wasn't surprised when he got right down to business. A newspaper was always on deadline. "So, Meg, what's going on with the murder there in Bramble? Anything fit to print?"

I took out my notebook and filled him in on the things Sally and I discussed the day before.

"What do the police have to say?" Harry asked. "Any leads?"

"Supposedly, they have a suspect." I omitted telling Harry my source was gossip overheard in Gloria's Glamour.

"Hmm. Well, let's hope it gets solved," said Harry. "Not that we don't have enough homicides to cover here in Chicago, but for your sake. I don't like the idea of some killer running around out there." I felt my eyes tear up. Harry had always looked out for me. He and his wife had no children, and his cub reporters were in many ways the family he never had.

He cleared his throat. "We need to talk about the next Miss Polly book." We spent the next couple of hours going over the columns I wrote since the last book. With Miss Polly handing out advice twice a week, we had about a thousand articles to review. Not that all of them were stellar, but we still had several hundred to cull from the backup diskettes. It would take more time than today's meeting.

"I think we've got a good start here, Meg," Harry said, rising to his feet. He reached across to one of the stacks of papers on his desk, pulled out a large manila envelope, and handed it to me. "Almost forgot. Here's a copy of the stuff we found in our archives about the Porter-Burton company."

"Thanks, Harry." Being careful to cover up the steamy novel I took from the train station, I wedged the envelope into my purse, and handed him the film from my camera.

"Let me know if anything more develops out there with the Burton case."

"Sure, Harry." I turned and made my way to the elevators.

I knew from his tone that Simon Burton's murder was cooling on the back burner of the *Journal*. Little did either of us know it would soon become red hot.

Chapter 16

Brad Trinder was in the lobby, browsing all of the plaques and awards the *Journal-Times* had won over the years.

He turned as I walked over to him. "You found your way here," I said.

"Yep. No problem. Just told the cabbie." Brad gave me an easy smile. "So, where are we off to? Mammoths? Sharks? Maybe lunch first?"

"Lunch sounds great. It's such a nice day. What would you think about having lunch near here? We can walk along the river."

"Fine with me. Is there something outside we can do afterward?" he asked. "Not that I'm against submarines and fossils."

I laughed. "I agree. No museums today." I thought for a moment. "I know! Have you ever been on an architectural tour of Chicago?"

"Architecture?"

"Chicago is world famous for its buildings: Mies van der Rohe, Bertrand Goldberg…"

"Would we get off the tour bus and look around?"

"No tour bus. Boat ride down the Chicago River."

"Wow! That sounds like fun!" Brad's enthusiasm showed in his eyes.

We strolled along the river to the River Trend Restaurant. It was crowded with office workers in shirtsleeves and tourists. However, the service was prompt, and we were soon enjoying wonderful sandwiches.

Time to be blunt. "Okay, Brad. Time for you to 'fess up. What is it you do at PBE?"

Brad slowly chewed the food in his mouth. "I'm an accountant."

"What?" My idea of an accountant did not line up with this good-looking man sitting across from me.

"Could be worse. I could be an actuary."
"What?"

"An inside joke in my trade. People become actuaries if they don't have the charisma to be an accountant."

I smiled. Brad had more charisma than he needed for bookkeeping. I needed to push aside my preconceptions and stereotypes. "Have you worked for PBE long?"

"Actually, I don't exactly work for PBE. I'm with an independent firm, auditing their finances in preparation for the Prairie Lake project. As with any big operation, the backers and lenders are concerned and want to make sure all's as it should be, financially."

He took a bite of his turkey and Brie wrap. "This is wonderful. Even has kale and sprouts in it."

Kale and sprouts? I thought of my peanut-butter-and-banana luncheon staple. I needn't have worried about Sally's "bash." He'd fit right in.

"Your turn," Brad said. "What's your position at the *Journal-Times*?"

"I keep this quiet, Brad, but I write the 'Ask Miss Polly' column."

He gave a low whistle. "I always thought some old biddy wrote it." He paused. "Gotcha! Another stereotype overturned. I know I don't seem like a bookkeeper type, and you sure don't look like an advice columnist. You look like…"

"A sophisticated waif." I told him about the episode at Gloria's Glamour.

"Why do women do this to themselves?" he asked.

"Glamor, dahlink, glamor," I replied.

Brad laughed and placed his hand over mine as I reached for my glass of water.

§

We were still laughing as we left the restaurant. Brad held my hand as we walked the few blocks to the *Wendella* dock. We had only a few minutes to wait before the next excursion.

The boat meandered down the Chicago River. I was glad I'd worn a jacket, as it was cooler on the water. Our guide pointed out the buildings we passed, adding anecdotes about them and their designers. I'd taken this tour before, but was still impressed by the variety of architectural styles clustered in downtown Chicago. How often I had walked by them, oblivious to their grandeur and history?

"I had no idea," Brad said several times.

The tour concluded in a little over an hour, and we disembarked.

Brad turned to me. "If we're going to Bramble tonight, it's about time to catch a cab over to the train station." *If* we're going to Bramble tonight? I must have looked startled, as he said nothing more and hailed a passing taxicab.

On the train, we talked about the buildings on the tour, pointing out items in the brochures we'd picked up. Brad walked me to my car. He bent down and kissed me softly. "Thank you, Meg. This was a day I'll always remember."

"Me too, Brad."

§

I replenished Minerva's food, thought about dinner for myself, but decided instead to take a shower and sort through thoughts about Brad. I climbed into bed, where the early start to the day and the fresh air on the river soon overcame me. Like Scarlett O'Hara, I'd think about it tomorrow.

Chapter 17

Tuesday. Two days before my parents arrived. Two days to shovel out my house and shop for real food. No peanut butter and bananas. I smiled and thought of Brad; no kale or sprouts either. I dabbed what I now thought of as "Gloria's Goo" into my hair in a vain attempt to control the scores of cowlicks that had appeared overnight, pulled on a pair of jeans and a T-shirt, and went downstairs. As I nibbled some toast, I made a list of things to do. Given a choice between shopping for food and cleaning the house, the groceries always won.

No way was I going to the Basket O'Bargains for a large amount of groceries. The bill would be such that I'd fulfill my mother's prophecy and be eating cat food—gourmet, of course—by the light of a solitary candle. On the way to Henry's, the grocery store out on the Interstate, I'd drop off the romance novel at the motel for Claudie.

§

After parking my car in front of the Interstate Sleepytime Motel office, I took the paperback book from the passenger seat, and went inside. Claudie, clenching a pencil between her teeth, was sorting stacks of papers on her desk. I waited at the counter, not wanting to disturb her concentration. A thin brochure on the counter promoting the joys of living in Florida caught my eye. I picked it up, and looked at photos of clear skies, ocean waves, and palm trees. Not an alligator in sight.

Claudie took the pencil out of her mouth, placed her hands on her hips, and heaved a sigh. She noticed me standing at the counter. "Oh, hi. Have you been here long?" She gestured to the piles on her desk. "Trying to get some order to all this. I have Babsy Wilcox come in every now and then to help out, answer the phones and such, but filing is not her strong suit."

Claudie walked over to the counter. I handed her the pamphlet. She took it and said, "Max will never leave here." She gave another sigh. "But I can still dream. Just a vacation once in a while would be nice." She opened a drawer behind the counter, shoved in the leaflet, and pushed the drawer shut. "You didn't come in here to listen to me go on and on," Claudie continued, "What can I do ya for?"

I handed her the romance novel. "I was at the train station and saw this in their bin. I thought if you didn't have it in your collection…" I nodded to the shelf of books. "I'm on the way to Henry's, so this was a good chance to drop it off." My words sounded lame, even to me.

"Well, aren't you sweet?" From her tone, I couldn't tell whether she was being sarcastic.

"I saw Marlene Tigran's name in one of the books when I was here with Sally Montrose. Are you and Marlene friends? Maybe she could help you out once in a while when you're swamped here."

Claudie laughed. "Oh, Marlene works here from time to time."

"Guess I'd best be going," I said. "My parents are coming in for a visit, and I need to have some food on hand besides TV dinners."

"Where do they live?"

"In Arizona. They retired there."

"Lucky them." Claudie smiled. "Thanks for the book. See you at the Montrose party."

I got into my car, started it up, and thought about the gun I'd seen in Claudie's drawer.

§

Henry's is a typical supermarket. Muscles straining, I separated a grocery cart from the dozens jammed together inside the door, and took out my shopping list. As I gazed around the produce department, with its abundance of fruits and vegeta-vegetables overflowing the stands, I thought, as I often did, how obscene it is to have so much while so many in the world have so little.

Shopping for my parents' visits is always a challenge. I need to have something already on hand for them to eat, and also some things for Mom to cook. She's a crazy-good cook—not gourmet, exactly, but guaranteed to plump up even the fussiest of eaters. I managed to get through the store in under an hour—not counting the checkout line moving at glacial speed.

After unpacking my groceries at home, I braved possible withdrawal symptoms and made myself a sandwich of something other than peanut butter and bananas—peanut butter and jelly.

I hauled out my cleaning supplies, and began the odious chores of wiping, scrubbing, sweeping, polishing, and vacuuming. Minerva, her tail puffed out, hissed at the vacuum, and fled to parts unknown.

The afternoon wore on and I wore out. After a long, hot shower, I looked inside the refrigerator, the pantry, and several cabinets. How could I have spent so much money, dragged home so much food, and still have nothing for dinner? I dialed Rosario's Pizza.

§

My body tired, but my stomach full, I sprawled on the couch, and tried to organize my thoughts about the murder. I didn't get far. Thoughts of Brad Trinder kept intruding. I admitted I was attracted to him. He was bright, funny, handsome. He even liked my new haircut. But who is he? What did I know about him? I roused the cat, who had curled up on my lap, and searched out a pencil and paper. Returning to the couch, I started a list:

• Accountant hired to audit PBE. Something amiss with PBE?

• Has a *pied-à-terre* in Chicago. Where is his home?

• Convention where he met Craig? Do accountants and investment brokers attend the same conventions?

I stopped. A guy asks me on a date. We go out and have fun. Now I'm making a list about him? Good grief. I put my notes aside and stretched out again. Maybe I was paranoid, or as my mother would say, "A girl can't be too careful."

Or was I was trying to find fault in Brad to avoid a romantic entanglement? And what did he mean by "If we're going to Bramble tonight?" Did Brad think I'd just hop into bed with him? I laughed to myself. It wouldn't be the first time. After all, I was in college during the "make love, not war" days of the 1970s.

§

Matt Harrison came into my life when he was a law student at Northwestern University. He was only an inch or two taller than I, with blue eyes and unruly brown hair always in need of a haircut.

Ours was a prosaic beginning, a blind date arranged by mutual friends—dinner and a movie—except we never got to the movie. The restaurant—a pizza and beer joint filled with law students—was abuzz. The United States had invaded Grenada, after a bloody coup in which a Cuban-trained military force overthrew Grenada's government. Heated debates raged among the students: was President Reagan's primary motive protecting about a thousand U.S. civilians in Grenada, or was he using their safety as an excuse to curb Communism in the Caribbean?

Matt and I didn't agree on the politics of the Grenada invasion, or, as it turned out, on politics in general. He was a conservative through and through, and I was a newly minted member of the Fourth Estate. It didn't seem to matter that night. We walked and talked, and ended up at an all-night diner, where we devoured omelets as the sun came up. We ended up in bed together.

We saw each other almost every day, arguing politics, and blissfully making up. We were young and in love, and so, a few weeks later, he moved from his scruffy two-room apartment into my scruffy two-room apartment near the NU campus north of the Loop. Matt grew up in Detroit, but didn't talk much about his family, from whom he was estranged. He completed his undergraduate work at Princeton, where he had a full scholarship from IBM. When with other people, even students, he affected an East Coast accent, which I found amusing until I realized he was desperate to hide what he felt was his inferior background.

Matt made *Law Review,* and was soon buried in intense, all-consuming legal research. I worked long hours at the paper, starting at the bottom rung as a stringer, writing up a variety of stories that the reporters couldn't or didn't want to cover—engagement announcements, obituaries, high-school sports, and the like. It was often near ten at night when I trudged up the stairs to our third-floor apartment, trying to enter quietly so as not to disturb him while he pored over the giant legal tomes spread out on our only table. I bought food, cooked for us, tidied our tiny living space, and enjoyed those rare times when Matt would look up from his yellow legal pads and say, "Let's get out of here."

Toward the end of his law-school days, he invited me to the prom—legal slang for a reception and dinner given by one of the top LaSalle Street law firms for candidates they had vetted and would likely ask to join their firm. Matt was still in bed that morning after a long session with the law books. I had a couple of deadlines at the paper that day, so we agreed to meet downtown at the exclusive Union League Club. I retrieved my all-purpose "little black dress" from the dry cleaners and changed into it in the ladies' room at my office, fussed with my makeup and hair, and donned my high heels. It had been months since the last time I wore heels, so by the time I reached the *Journal* lobby, my feet rebelled. It was a twenty-minute walk to the reception, so I splurged on a cab ride to avoid limping into the reception.

As I entered the club, a gentleman greeted me at the door, asked for my invitation, and directed me to the main dining room. I reached the doorway and paused, amazed. To say the room was elegant would be an understatement. Crystal chandeliers sparkled from the high ceiling with what appeared to be hand-stenciled beams. Fan-light windows and walnut-trimmed walls showcased artwork. I walked over to the nearest picture.

As I admired it, I heard Matt's voice behind me. "Don't gawk, Meg."

I turned, a smile on my lips, which froze in the iciness of his stare.

"What were you thinking, wearing *that* dress?"

Taken aback, I looked down at my dress. "This is my best outfit, Matt."

"It's your *only* outfit. Couldn't you have gone shopping for something new? Maybe squeeze it in between bridal write-ups? You knew tonight is important to me."

"None of these people have seen this dress before. I don't see what's wrong with it." His sarcasm stung me, although I refrained from pointing out that there was no money for a new dress. I was the one who bought groceries and paid the bills. I even gave him the money for the Michigan Avenue haircut he was sporting.

"Look around," Matt said. He waved his hand at the groups of people talking quietly around the room. I was under-dressed. All the women were in glitzy gowns, the men in dark suits, and a few in black-tie.

"Maybe I should leave," I suggested.

"Yes. You should. I'll tell them you were suddenly taken ill."

Tears blinding my eyes, I wheeled around and left the room.

§

That was a long time ago, in the wild 1970s, not that I've remained celibate these twenty-some years. I admit I wouldn't mind seeing Brad again, casually. But I needed to know more about him.

Chapter 18

A stream of sunlight trickled through the living-room blinds and played on my eyelids. After my run to the motel yesterday, followed by shopping, cleaning, and sating my appetite with pizza last night, it was no wonder that I'd fallen asleep on the couch. I got to my feet, stretched, and folded the afghan I'd cuddled up with. All in all, I felt pretty good.

My face did not share that opinion. The mirror showed a woman whose face had deep pad marks from the couch. My skin resembled a relief map of a great river system. A shower and globs of moisturizer helped smooth out or, perhaps, fill in, most of the crevices.

As I browsed through the morning *Journal,* Minerva jumped on the table and tried to lap milk from my cereal. "I don't do this when you're eating," I scolded, and lifted her gently to the floor. Mom is coming here tomorrow, and I don't suppose there's enough time to train Minerva to stay off the counters and tables. "Had we but world enough and time," as the poet said.

I spent the morning cleaning up the yard. The grass needed mowing, but I knew Dad would want to do it—partly to feel useful, partly to get out of the house when Mom took over the kitchen. I hosed down the dock, cleaned out the kayak, and dug out a few weeds. I heard the phone ring and dashed inside, kicking off my muddy shoes next to the door.

"Hello," I panted.

"Hi," came a familiar voice.

"Hi, Brad."

"You're out of breath. I had no idea I had such an effect on you." He laughed.

I ignored his comment. "Been puttering around outside. My parents are coming in tomorrow."

"Oh, right. You mentioned that the other day." He paused. "Which is why I called. I had such a great time Monday, and so I wondered if you'd like to have dinner with me tonight at the Heron?"

"That sounds good. I'd like that," I said.

"How does seven o'clock sound? I'll pick you up."

"Fine with me. See you then."

My first thought as I walked over to the stairs? Thank goodness my house is clean. My second thought? Why did Minerva pick today to upchuck a hairball on the carpet?

§

As it so often does, time both dragged and flew by. I took another shower, and spent more time primping since…well, since Monday. The facial lines from my night on the couch were gone, and my new haircut was beginning to behave. I looked one more time into the full-length mirror in the hall. "Not bad, old girl. Not bad," I told the reflection.

Brad arrived at seven. Hoping he didn't notice the wet spot and lingering odor of Smell Sweet on the carpet, I showed him into the living room while I closed the windows and made sure Minerva wasn't locked in a closet by accident. When I came back, he turned, a photograph in his hand. "Are these your parents?"

"Yes. That picture was taken the last time I visited them in Arizona."

"You look a lot like your mother."

"Thanks. I definitely take that as a compliment."

Brad held the door of his white Porsche open for me, then got in effortlessly, especially for a man his height. No wonder he had no trouble riding in my car when Simon's body was discovered.

Aloud, I said, "Great car!"

"Do you like sports cars?"

"Sure do."

He nodded. "I like tinkering with cars, so this is fun for me on both levels." He glanced over at me and smiled. "Another blow to the accountant stereotype."

I laughed. "No four-door beige sedan for you, huh?"

"In the practical desert-sand color."

"With bench seats," we both said at once.

§

The Heron was full for a Wednesday evening. Louis seated us in a booth in a quiet corner, handed us menus, and took our drink orders.

"Where do you do all the oil changes and things on your Porsche?" Perhaps I could find out more about Brad with a subtle approach. "Do you have a garage?"

Brad looked at me, and said, "What is it you really want to know, Meg?"

Guess my subtlety didn't work. I busied myself with my menu, trying to formulate a reply. When I looked up, his eyes were still on me. The words from my list the night before came tumbling from my mouth. "I guess I'm ill at ease, Brad. You seem to be a good guy, and I like you, but I know nothing about you. For instance, where is your home? Is PBE in some sort of financial trouble? Did you..."

Brad raised his hands in mock defense. "Whoa! I'll confess."

"I'm not kidding."

"I know," he replied. "I didn't know at first whether I could trust you. I know that right now, you're more than Miss Polly. You were a damn good reporter for the *Journal-Times,* so it stands to reason that you aren't sitting around giving advice to the lovelorn when there's been a murder in town."

I bristled. "I don't just give advice to the lovelorn. Many of my readers are in serious trouble or in danger. I've referred dozens to safe houses, store-front law firms..."

"I'm sorry. That didn't come out quite right. Anyway, am I correct in thinking you're doing some investigating for the paper?"

"Yes, I am," I straightened up. "But that doesn't answer my questions about you."

Louis set down our drinks: a glass of wine for me, scotch and water for Brad. "What would you like tonight?"

Brad ordered the filet mignon with porcini mushroom butter, which sounded good to me too.

"So two filets. Medium-rare okay? Cauliflower au gratin comes with it," said Louis.

Brad looked at me. I nodded. "Same for both of us. Thanks." Louis picked up our menus and departed for the kitchen.

"So, man of mystery, who are you?" I asked.

"What I tell you is off the record. We...I can't have any of this known by your editors or anyone else," he replied.

"You can trust me, Brad."

He was silent for a moment, and then said, "Meg, I'm a forensic accountant. Porter-Burton Enterprises thinks that a group of minority shareholders scraped up enough money to have me come in to audit their books.”

“A forensic accountant? You mean you investigate things like fraud?”

“That’s right.”

“So who do you actually work for?” I pressed.

“I’m a special agent with the FBI.”

“Holy…”

“I get that a lot,” Brad chuckled. He smiled and reached for my hand. “I hope this doesn’t affect our relationship, Meg.”

Relationship? My head was still processing the idea of Brad being an FBI agent, let alone…relationship? I moved my hand from his and reached for my wine, resisting the urge to chug it.

Recovering a few of my wits, I said, “But then, where do you live? Washington?”

“Right now, the condo in Chicago is home. The government owns it, keeps it for people like me who need to have temporary lodging when on assignment. I did have a home in Maryland…” His voice trailed off.

“Oh?”

"My wife and I parted company a few years ago. Being an agent isn't the best ingredient of a happy marriage."

I thought it best to move our conversation away from his divorce, so I asked, "Does Craig know that you're, um…"

"An FBI agent? Yes. And before you ask, I didn't meet Craig accidentally at the convention last year. I arranged to talk with him about assisting us with a few things. He has an excellent reputation. Investment people are often helpful in unraveling financial situations I deal with. Craig is especially helpful since he has clients all over the globe."

Our steaks arrived, sizzling on platters, putting pause to our conversation. As delicious as the dinner was, it didn't divert my thoughts from spinning through my head.

§

Brad and I passed on dessert, but lingered over snifters of brandy after dinner. Our conversation seemed to add another dimension to our friendship. Or relationship. Or whatever this was between us. As we were getting up to leave, we both spotted the couple seated at a table across the room from us: Travis Burton and Susanne Porter.

"Have they been there all evening?" I asked Brad.

"Using my extraordinary powers of deduction, I'd say not. Looks like they've about finished the salad course."

As we watched, Susanne ran her hand up Travis's leg under the table. Sally's scuttlebutt from Paula at the beauty shop was on target.

"And using *my* extraordinary powers gained through years of giving advice to the lovelorn," I joked, "I'd bet they're not discussing the weather or the next Bears game."

§

Brad and I scurried out of the restaurant before Travis and Susanne saw us. Not much danger of that, given the steamy looks the two were exchanging.

In the car, I said, "I thought Susanne had arrived the day after Simon's murder to arrange for Simon's remains and all." I didn't dare mention I learned that while hiding among the velvet folds of the Memory Meadows draperies. Another instance of protecting my sources.

"She and Travis were here when I arrived," Brad said. "I rented that Lincoln for Travis Burton, and met him at the funeral home with it. When he asked me to extend the rental period, I knew he was staying on in Bramble," said Brad, "and since we're all staying at the hotel in town, I couldn't help but see Susanne was still here. To be honest, there's been something going on between them for a while now."

"Edwin Burton's at the hotel, too, right?"

Brad nodded.

I said, "I wonder if he suspects…anything." I caught myself just in time, before I used the term "hanky-panky."

"Bramble is a good place for them to, er, meet. No one from the city would see them. And, of course, being in the same hotel…"

§

I asked Brad to come in for a nightcap. "What would you like?" I asked, quickly adding when I saw him wiggle his eyebrows, "To eat." That wasn't much better.

He grinned. "This is an odd request, I know, but do you have any ice cream?"

"No ice cream, but I do have this wonderful frozen yogurt. Chocolate with peanut butter chunks in it."

"Sounds great."

"Coffee?"

"Sure. Regular or decaf is fine. Whatever you're having. Caffeine doesn't bother me."

Brad followed me out to the kitchen, and sat at the bare table, its top empty of papers in preparation for my mother's descent the next day. I fiddled with the coffee pot and took the yogurt from the freezer. I kept sneaking looks at him. Dear God, he's good-looking. I pictured his lips on mine, his—

My salacious thoughts were interrupted. "Let me help," Brad said, rising a bit from his chair and reaching across the table for the yogurt container.

I clattered around in the cabinet under the sink, fished out a tray, and began to load it to carry things for our almost-midnight snack into the dining room. "Don't bother," Brad said. "Let's eat here in the kitchen." He lowered himself back into his chair. And sat on the cat.

§

Both Minerva and Brad survived the encounter. I now know what a caterwaul sounds like. Minerva screeched, clawed her way out from under Brad's backside, and jumped on the table, spilling hot coffee on Brad's front side.

Masculine pride and a high pain tolerance must have kept Brad from screeching too. I grabbed some clean rags, wet them, and began dabbing him, ineffectually, here and there. This was not exactly how I pictured the evening to end.

I gave Brad some towels to place in the car so his wet pants wouldn't ruin the soft leather upholstery. He moved gingerly. His entry into the car wasn't as effortless as earlier in the evening, but he gave the horn a couple of light taps as he drove away. And a good time was had by all.

I shut the door, and went into the kitchen to finish cleaning up the mess. Minerva, her eyes inscrutable as ever, was perched on the table, running her tongue over her whiskers, cleaning off traces of coffee cream. I couldn't help but chuckle, thinking back on my fussing and fretting over the nature of my "relationship" with Brad. So much for that. I turned out the lights and went up to bed.

Chapter 19

Around ten in the morning, a dark green Plymouth sedan and a black Chevy SUV pulled up in front of my house. Bert Schmidt, owner of Bert's Rent-a-Car, handed me the keys to the SUV and made me sign my life away in return, before he left in the second car driven by one of his employees. I always rented a van or SUV to pick up my folks when they came in for a visit, as my Celica would never hold them and their luggage.

Their flight wasn't due in at O'Hare until late afternoon, so I climbed into the rental car and drove over to Sally's house to see if there was anything I could help her with for the open house.

The Heron's catering van was pulled up next to the side door, so I went in through the open doorway. I heard voices from the kitchen, and started toward them. Jon Dreher and Sally seemed deep in conversation, and I paused in the back hallway, uncertain as to what to do. As I stood there, I heard Jon say, "…vicious man. He stopped by our house recently. Louis didn't happen to be home at the time. Burton kept hinting that Louis was with someone else, some young guy staying at the hotel in town. I know Burton wanted to drive a wedge between us so we'd split up and sell our home to PBE, but I can't seem to forget what he said." Jon was about twelve years older than Louis, but there had never been a whisper about any infidelity on the part of either of them.

Sally asked, "Have you talked with Louis about this?"

"How can I bring it up without looking like I distrust him? We're flying to Copenhagen this winter."

I didn't hear Sally reply, but she must've indicated interest, because Jon continued, "Gay marriage is illegal everywhere, but we can have a civil union ceremony performed in Denmark."

"Oh, Jon, that would be wonderful. I'm so pleased for both of you. But—"

"I know, I know. I need to talk soon with Louis."

I heard the scrape of chairs being moved, and quickly called out, "Hello? Anyone here?"

"In here, Meg," Sally answered. "Jon's setting up for Saturday's party."

I stepped into Sally's enormous kitchen, which was dominated by a twelve-foot-long plank farm table in the center, piled high today with cartons and bags bearing the Heron logo. The kitchen was cozy and inviting, despite its institutional eight-burner stove with two ovens and a refrigerator large enough to hold enough food to feed the entire population of Bramble. Craig confided to me over our drinks a few days ago that Sally was coming close to doing that, as her invitation list continued to grow.

"Hi, Sally, Jon," I said. "I thought I'd stop by and see if there's anything you need doing. I have to pick up my folks at O'Hare this afternoon, but I have some time now."

Jon was dressed in jeans and a tight T-shirt. I'd forgotten how muscular he was. "Hi, Meg. Thanks for the offer, but a couple of my busboys are coming by to help put things together, earn a little extra money. By the way, did you and Mr. Trinder like your steaks last night? I was trying out that new sauce."

I felt Sally trying to catch my eye. "Everything was great, Jon. Another wonderful meal."

He beamed and went out the door.

Sally looked around me to make sure Jon was gone. Her eyes flashed with merriment. "Brad Trinder? Last night?" She struck a fortune-teller's pose. "And do you have something to tell Madam Sally?"

"How much time do you have?" I asked, hoping she was too busy to hear my tale of woe.

"Sit down and start talking."

After a few minutes, Craig came up the basement stairs, stuck his head around the door, and said, "I thought I heard a lot of giggling. Can I come in or are you two having a cat session?"

We howled. "A-a cat session!"

Craig shook his head, got a Coke out of the refrigerator, and went back to his office.

§

Still weak from laughter, I drove home and scrutinized my house one last time, especially the kitchen, scene of last night's fiasco. I started for the airport. I always park my car in the short-term lot and meet my parents at the gate so I can help them navigate the vast "world's busiest airport." I allowed plenty of time to get there and was early, so I bought a cup of coffee and sat at the gate to wait.

For the first time I can remember, their flight was on time. My parents were among the first two hundred people off the giant plane. In common with all the other passengers, they looked a bit bewildered as they entered the terminal, as if they had landed here by accident on their way to another galaxy. They saw me, waved, and walked over. Hugs all around. It was good to see them.

Mom matched me pace-for-pace as we followed the crowds to the baggage claim area. Dad, as usual, took in everything around him, even reading directional signs, and brought up the rear. Mom dressed all in tan, a style I called—not to her face, of course—Sun Belt Safari. Her cargo pants had cunning zippers on the thighs so that they could be converted into longish shorts at a moment's notice. Mom's blouse was in the same fabric, with long sleeves that could be pushed up and held with a snap. Both garments were made of a fabric that the outfitter stores promised had the ability to "wick away" moisture. That seemed strange, there being little moisture in the desert, and perspiration, if it appeared at all, evaporated before it could depart to wherever wicked-away wetness went. In contrast with her big-game hunting apparel, Mom wore a broad-brimmed straw hat and carried an enormous straw bag, covered with appliquéd cacti and lizards.

She talked without ceasing, bringing me up to date on cousins seventeen times removed and gossip about other residents of their retirement community. She was bright and pert for having been on an airplane for several hours. Her round face was a little more lined, and the exposure to the sun had darkened ("bronzed," as Mom would say) her face and arms.

Dad caught up to us at the baggage carousel. In contrast to Mom, he looked pale. He wore slacks and a sport shirt with a cardigan sweater zipped up about halfway to his throat. His spare frame seemed thinner than I remembered, and he was a bit out of breath after he hauled in their first suitcase. Three more pieces of luggage followed. I was glad I thought to snag a cart. I wheeled the cart to the terminal exit and arranged to pick them up outside. I eyed the luggage piled on the cart. Did they leave anything in Arizona? They were only staying three nights.

As we sped along the Interstate highways, Mom sat up front with me, while Dad sat in the back. Soon his head was back and he was sound asleep. I shot an inquiring look at Mom, who pursed her lips into a thin line, shook her head, and mouthed, "Later."

§

By the time we arrived home, it was dinnertime, or suppertime, as the Bramble natives call it. Dad stretched and yawned, and started unloading the suitcases. Before he could stop me, I grabbed a couple, and schlepped them upstairs to the guest room. He and I managed the other two, then went down to the kitchen where Mom was already peering into the refrigerator.

"I'll make a salad, Mom. As long as you're in there, take out the blue bowl. I made that chicken casserole you and Dad like. Thought we'd heat it up and have it for dinner."

I took the casserole from her and placed it in the oven. "Mom, remember when I was a kid, and you always made that awful tuna casserole?"

"It wasn't 'always,' and it wasn't that awful." Mom smiled. "I put crushed potato chips on top."

"It didn't help. Just a waste of good potato chips."

"How sharper than a serpent's tooth it is to have a thankless child!"

Not many mothers can, or would, quote from *King Lear* in ordinary conversation. Mom was a retired English teacher, and the primary source of my love of words and writing. I gave her a hug. "I'm so glad you and Dad are here."

"Hey, can I get in on that hug?" Dad came into the room. He looked better. The nap in the car must've helped.

"Sure can," I said. Mom and I opened our arms and wrapped them around him.

"I think I'll go outside and poke around," he said.

"Don't get involved in anything," said Mom. "We'll be eating soon."

He ambled outside. I asked Mom, "Is Dad okay? He seems thinner, and a bit out of breath sometimes."

"His chain-smoking finally caught up with him."

"He hasn't smoked in years," I said.

"Doesn't matter, the doctor said. He's got the beginnings of emphysema." Glancing at me, she continued, "Now don't go worrying about it, Meg. Phoenix has wonderful care for people with lung problems. He sees a specialist regularly and is taking much better care of himself. And don't mention your concerns to him. You know how he is about illness."

"I guess so. Always had to be strong," I said.

"Especially around his little girl." She smiled. "Go on outside. I'll do the salad and keep an eye on the oven."

Dad was on the dock, gazing at a pair of swans that were floating by in graceful beauty. "Pretty, aren't they, Dad? I don't know if they're lovelier swimming or flying. Definitely odd to see them waddling on land."

"They're not native here, are they?" he asked.

"I don't think so. Companies buy them to decorate their retention ponds, but forget to clip their wings. So the feathers grow back, and the birds are free. Supposedly, they do well in the winter, although I haven't seen them then."

"I thought swans were supposed to keep the geese from nesting," Dad said.

"Not here. Canada geese and the swans swim around together, but I doubt if they get near each other's nests."

We sat quietly for a while. "Let's dig up some night crawlers and go fishing tomorrow morning," he suggested.

"It's a date." I took the small, red pail I kept on the dock, and went to get a shovel from my shed. Dad and I shoveled the soft earth under the scarlet maple until Mom called us in.

After we scrubbed our hands at the sink in the powder room downstairs, we sat down at the kitchen table. The idea of using the dining room for our meals never occurred to Mom or me. Kitchen was family. Kitchen was home.

§

After dinner, the three of us sat in the living room and chatted. The moment came that I'd dreaded.

"So, Meg, are you dating anyone?" asked Mom.

"Helen, for heaven's sake. Leave Meg alone," Dad said.

"That's okay, Dad."

My parents were bound to meet Brad at Sally's party, so I figured it was best to come clean. Almost clean. "I had dinner with a nice man last night. His name's Brad. He's in town for a while. Something to do with the proposed development of Cottage Row." There was no way I would tell Mom and Dad that I was dating an FBI agent who was here investigating PBE. I was sworn to silence about that anyway.

"What does he do for a living?"

"He's an accountant, Mom."

"Will he be at Sally's and Craig's party?"

"Probably. They've invited practically the whole town."

Because neither of my folks had mentioned the murder, I knew they hadn't heard about it in Arizona. However, they certainly would learn about it at the Montrose party, so I took a deep breath, and plunged in. "Speaking of the development, we've had some excitement here. One of the owners of the construction company was killed."

"Oh, that's too bad," Mom said. "Was it an accident?"

"Um, well, no. Someone killed him."

Dad sat up straight and asked, "You mean, on purpose?"

I tried to downplay it. "The police think so."

"Oh, Meg," Mom said. "We were so glad when you left Chicago. We thought you'd be safe here."

"Mom, please don't worry. I *am* safe here."

Chapter 20

The smell of bacon woke me the next morning. I looked at the clock. After nine. Late for me. I was surprised that Minerva hadn't become impatient for breakfast. I brushed my teeth, donned my ratty bathrobe, and went downstairs.

I needn't have worried about my feline companion. Mom had fed her. As I traipsed into the kitchen, Minerva was busy scarfing down a dish of the gourmet cat food she deigned not to touch the other day.

"Good morning, dear," my mother said. Dad nodded at me from over the top of the morning *Journal-Times.* Both of my parents were already dressed.

"Have you been up for long?" I asked, as I removed a container of orange juice from the refrigerator.

"Oh, about an hour or so," Mom said. "We're usually up and at 'em by eight in Phoenix. Different time zone here."

§

While I got dressed, Dad went outside and got out two poles and the tackle box from the shed. He carried them and the pail of worms we dug the night before to my aluminum canoe.

As I walked through the kitchen on my way to join him, my mother reached over to the counter and held out a small hamper. "Just in case you get hungry, I've made a couple of sandwiches." My chances of getting hungry with my mother around were about the same as my chances of winning the Irish Sweepstakes.

Outside, I joined Dad, who was climbing into the canoe. He moved more stiffly than I remembered from their last visit, but so do I, for that matter. We settled our gear, and used our paddles to push off from the shore into Prairie Lake.

The surface of the lake was glassy, marred only by the squiggles of water bugs and our own progress through the water. The sun promised a pleasant day, but in that way early autumn has of underlying the warmth with a slight chill. The trees along the water were already aflame with color, hinting at an early winter.

We baited our hooks, sat back on the cushions that doubled as floatation devices, and smiled at each other. A glorious day.

After a few minutes, Dad said, "There's something more about this Brad fellow, isn't there?"

"I doubt if it's going anywhere after last night."

"What happened last night, Meg? He didn't hurt you, did he?"

"Oh, Dad! Nothing like that. He was the one hurt—by Minerva."

"Minerva?"

"Yep. It started with a really nice steak dinner…"

We laughed and talked for a couple of more hours, then attacked the hamper of food Mom had prepared. "I don't know how she does it," I said, chomping on a chicken-salad sandwich. "I had this food in the house, but would never have thought about putting it together like this."

"She's a talented woman, your mother," Dad replied. "She's keeping an eye on my eating habits." He patted his waist. "If I get any skinnier, I'll be transparent."

We tugged the canoe up on the shore, and turned it over. After we put the fishing gear away, we went inside with the empty hamper.

"Hey, Mom! We're back!" I yelled.

"No need to yell. I'm here in the living room."

Dad and I joined her.

"Did you catch anything?" she asked.

"Nope."

"Good. I hate cleaning fish."

We laughed.

"Walt," she said, "Why don't you take a bit of a rest?"

"Maybe later."

"Maybe now."

"Yes, dear," Dad said, winking at me. "I'll go upstairs, clean myself up a bit, and catch up on my reading."

I went to the kitchen to wash our picnic things. As I was putting the plastic plates in the dishwasher, my mother stalked in. "I didn't want to upset your father," she said, "but I found these when I was tidying up your living room."

In her hand, Mom flourished my notes about Simon Burton's murder. My stomach lurched.

"You are much more involved in this than you let on, aren't you?"

I nodded.

"And most of these people are going to be at the party tomorrow, aren't they?"

I nodded again.

"Aren't you afraid to be in the same room with a murderer?"

I made no reply. Right now, I was more afraid to be in the same room with my mother.

"I'll keep my eyes and ears open at the party," Mom said. "Who knows? I may learn something that will help solve the murder."

Swell. Just what I needed: Mom the detective. Brad, Sally, me, and now Mom. Bramble was awash in investigators. There is no arguing with my mother once she's set on something, so I gave her a bleak nod, and went upstairs to get ready for the Montrose party.

Chapter 21

My parents and I purposely arrived a bit early at the open house, so we could help Sally with any last-minute tasks. Dad went off to find Craig. Mom headed for the kitchen, of course, and I trailed along after her. Sally gave a little wave as we walked in. She looked wonderful in a knit dress in a deep rust color, cinched at the waist with a large belt with a bronze buckle of intricate design. She wore high heels, even though she'd be on her feet all day.

"How can we help?" I asked.

Sally walked over and squeezed both of Mom's hands in hers. "So good to see you again, Mrs. Smyth. Arizona must agree with you. You look wonderful."

"Sally, so good of you to ask us to your party," Mom said, "but you haven't answered Meg's question. Can we help? Put us to work."

"Not much left to do, thank you. Jon and Louis have been here since early this morning with their workers. Go on in and keep Craig from monopolizing your father. I'll be out in a minute."

Mom took my arm, and led me from the kitchen and into the dining room. I had heard the expression, "groaning board," before, but never had actually seen one. The dining-room table and sideboard were laden with food: appetizers, small sandwiches, and desserts. The focal point of the table was a mountainous ice sculpture with the words, "Hurray!" cut into it. Glass plates and linen napkins were at one end of the table, along with silverware. No paper plates and plastic cutlery for Sally. Workers from the Heron balanced huge trays of goodies as they hustled from kitchen to dining room in orderly chaos.

We joined Craig and Dad in the living room—or parlor, as Sally would say—trying their best to stay out of the way of the caterers who were setting up and adding linen covers to folding chairs in the room. A few moments later, Sally swept through the room on her way to answer a knock at the door. Craig rose and joined her to greet guests.

Ben and Nina Fulton entered, Nina leaning on a cane. Ben assisted Nina to a chair, turned, and left the house. Seeing our puzzled looks, Nina explained, "He's gone to get Gita and Tony Banicki. We thought it might be easier for her to manage in our van. Seems silly for us all to drive over here, anyway. Save a bit on gas."

Mom said, "I've noticed gasoline is cheaper here than in Phoenix. A little over a dollar a gallon." She and Nina were off on a conversation about the joys of living in Arizona, with Nina defending, in her pleasant way, the advantages of Bramble. I looked up to see Sally ushering in some more guests: Jake and Marlene Tigran.

I almost didn't recognize Jake. He was wearing a dark suit. Although about ten years out of fashion, it was clean and fit him well. His white shirt was new, the creases from the package evident on the collar. No red cap. And miracle of miracles, his cheek wasn't bulging with a plug of chewing tobacco.

Jake looked presentable, but Marlene was stunning. Her luxuriant coppery hair was combed over her ears, setting off gold hoop earrings set with green stones that sparkled as she moved. Her dark-green dress was unadorned, almost to the point of plainness, which somehow emphasized her shapely body.

As the Tigrans talked with Craig and Sally inside the front door, I'd never seen Marlene so animated. Max and Claudie Trent arrived and exchanged greetings with the four at the door. Marlene's face froze. There was no mistaking her expression. Fear. Who was Marlene afraid of? Max? Claudie? As for the Trents, either they didn't notice Marlene's reaction or were unfazed by it. Marlene grabbed Jake's hand, and pulled him out of the entryway. The Tigrans stopped in front of Nina, Mom, and me, and chatted for a bit. Actually, Jake did the chatting. Marlene appeared carved from marble. Jake spotted the dining room spread. He leaned over to me and whispered, "Are we allowed to eat now?" I advised him to wait a while until more guests were present. The couple moved to a couple of folding chairs across the room from where the Trents had seated themselves.

I looked over at Max and Claudie. Max had on a checked sport jacket that he wisely left unbuttoned over his girth, and Claudie wore a nice-looking, but somewhat dated, flowered dress. They were talking with some people who had come in while I was conversing with Jake. The room was filling. A buzz of conversation swelled in volume. Craig was right. Sally had invited almost the whole town.

Ben Fulton returned with Tony and Gita Banicki. Tony helped his mother into an armchair, and hovered over her, before sitting down next to her. I excused myself, gave my chair to Ben, and walked over to the Banickis. There was another chair nearby, which I moved over to the other side of Tony. "Hello, Tony, Mrs.—Gita," I said.

"Hello, dear," said Gita. "I know you, don't I?

"Yes. We met a few days ago at your house. I'm Meg Smyth."

"I have glorious hair—no, that's not right, Gloria's hair…" she stopped, patting her fluffy halo of white hair, which looked newly permed.

"Your hair looks beautiful," I said, truthfully. "Gloria did a wonderful job."

"Thank you, dear," Gita said.

"Mother, may I get you something to eat? Some punch?" asked Tony.

"Yes, Tony, that would be lovely."

When Pastor Joe, who was sitting on the other side of Gita, engaged her in conversation, I took the opportunity to excuse myself and headed for the array of food. Russ Banks, the barber, peeked around the ice sculpture and winked at me. He shook his head, and pointed to my hair. I gestured that I would be back at the Clipper Snip forthwith. Joe pointed to the "Hurrah!" carved in the ice.

I moved into the food line behind Tony Banicki.

"I'm so glad I had a chance to get to know your mother a little better. Even though we live just on the same street, and I see you rowing by almost every day…"

"She doesn't get out much. Being able to come to this party is a quite an accomplishment for her. She's talked about it for days. Her memory is not as good as it was, of course, but, considering what she's been through…"

Before Tony could lapse into silence, I seized the opportunity to inquire, "She was in a concentration camp, wasn't she? I saw the tattoo on her arm the other day."

Tony sighed. "Yes. When Germany occupied Poland, the Nazis took both my father and mother to a camp. A few weeks before, some of their friends who ran an underground network were able to smuggle me out. Before the network was discovered, that is. Mother never heard what happened to the people who helped so many of us kids.

"I was placed with a family, the Bensons, in the north of England. Both have passed away. They were kind, kept me safe, and made sure I got an education. They treated me like they would their own son, if they had one. They were Anglicans, of course, but there were a few other refugee Jews in the area, and the Bensons made sure I got to know them so I could grow up in my faith." Tony was almost chatty. Probably doesn't talk much outside his classroom at the college.

"How did you become reunited with your parents?" I asked.

"My father died in the camp. I never learned if it was from conditions or if he was...exterminated." Tony looked away for a moment. I waited for him to go on.

"My mother was released when the Russians liberated Poland. She was broken and nearly dead from abuse and 'experiments' by the Nazi SS in the camp. She didn't speak for months afterward. When she was well enough, she found me through one of the agencies that was formed to try to locate lost children.

"I crewed for Oxford, so I was relatively easy to find once they knew where to look." Tony gave me a bleak smile. "Those years were the best of my life, although I wouldn't put it that way to Mother, of course. It's my turn now to protect her and keep her safe."

"You're a devoted son, Tony," I said. "She is lucky to have you."

The line inched forward, and Tony handed me a plate.

§

Anyone with a phobia about different foods touching on one dish would need years of therapy after looking at my plate. I wove my way with care through the partygoers. The party was in full swing. Everyone seemed to be talking at once. As is the case with open houses, seating was fluid. People came and went. Only Nina and Gita, due to their infirmities, were still in the same chairs, as was Tony, who was next to his mother.

As I stood looking for a place to land, I heard angry voices coming from the music room, on the other side of the hall, which ran the length of the house. I set my plate down on an occasional table, and edged toward the doorway, and looked across the hall. Standing to one side of the baby grand was Marlene Tigran.

"You must stop! It's finished," she said.

"Sure is," said Claudie Trent. She gave a nasty laugh. "Can't be much more finished than your lover being dead. What did he ever see in you, anyway?"

Lover? Simon Porter?

"Why don't you leave me alone? I don't have any more money to give you," said Marlene.

"Those gold earrings would look nice with a dress I have at home," said Claudie. "Did he give them to you? As payment?"

"Here, take them!" I heard them hit the bare floor with a soft tinkling sound.

Marlene stormed out, running into me, and nearly knocking us both to the floor.

I grabbed Marlene's arm. She tried to wrench it away, but I held on, and said, "Let's step outside for a minute, Marlene."

We walked down the hall and out to the patio in the back yard. Marlene shook with sobs. "What am I going to do?"

"Start from the beginning, Marlene," I suggested.

"O-okay. I met Simon when he stopped by our house to try to talk us into selling to his company."

I nodded. Simon Porter or Travis Burton had talked, one-on-one, with all of us on Cottage Row at one time or another.

"I don't know. He was so nice, so gentlemanly. I offered him a glass of wine, even though it was the afternoon. The kids were at school…" Another heaving sob. I waited. "I just couldn't do it, I mean, there, in the bed Jake and I…

"Simon came by the next day. I knew what I was doing, can't say I didn't. I put on this same dress," she looked down at it. "He suggested the motel, that he'd make all the arrangements, no one would see me." Marlene's voice trailed off.

"Did you see Simon often?"

"I thought I loved him, I guess. Even put a pot of flowers in front of the cabin we…"

"Does Jake know?"

"No!" said Marlene. "That's what Claudie keeps threatening me with."

"Have you paid her?"

"I don't have money of my own, just what Jake gives me for food and stuff, so I couldn't pay her much. She said it would 'feather her nest egg,' whatever that means."

I thought of Claudie's Florida brochure. "Go on, Marlene."

"I don't have more money to give her. Those earrings today were my mother's. Simon never paid me. I'm not a whore. I'm not!" She cried and snuffled some more, her eye make-up running in dark rivulets down her cheeks. "What am I going to do?"

"What do *you* think you should do?"

"I can't tell Jake. I can't."

"Would it help to talk it over with Pastor Joe?"

"Pastor Joe?" Marlene stared at me with horror. "I couldn't do that. I'd never be able to face him again."

Marlene brightened. "Isn't blackmailing someone illegal? Maybe I could threaten Claudie, say I'll tell the police."

"Marlene, reciprocal blackmail isn't a good idea."

"Yeah. I guess recip…what you said…wouldn't be good. I'd be just as bad as her."

Marlene and I walked back into the house, where I pointed her to the tiny half-bath off the butler's pantry, so she could compose herself.

What if Jake already knew about Marlene's affair with Simon Porter?

§

I walked back into the house, picking up my plate of food on the way. I looked around for a spot to sit and graze. As I stood there, I heard Brad's voice in my ear, "What I wouldn't give for a good cup of hot coffee."

I whirled around, catching my plate of food in time to avoid another fun-filled encounter with him. "How are you?" I asked.

"No blisters in front, no stitches behind," he laughed, "so I'm on the road to recovery. How's Minerva?"

"Before you even cleared the driveway, she was sitting up and taking nourishment— spilled coffee cream." I smiled. "Brad, I am so sorry…"

"I should've looked before I sat back down. I like cats, but I haven't been around them much. So, no harm done, well, except to my pride, maybe. Shall we find a place to sit?"

Judging by the furtive way they crept out of the room, Craig and Dad were on their way to Craig's man cave, so Brad and I sat in the chairs they vacated. As he unbuttoned his sport jacket, I looked for a holster. "Don't you have to pack a piece all the time?"

Brad laughed. "'Pack a piece?' I recommend fewer cop shows for you."

"Just like Gita Banicki," I said.

Brad looked puzzled. "What?"

I told him about my visit to the Banicki cottage, how Tony tried to limit his mother's TV viewing. I looked around to make sure no one overheard me and asked, "So, are you required to carry a gun?"

"We're supposed to carry a weapon at all times, unless we're given clearance not to."

"Did you have one the other night?"

"Yes."

"I didn't notice it."

"I had it strapped on my leg, under my pants, so you wouldn't have noticed it." He smiled wolfishly. "That's where it is now. Wanna see?"

Feeling my face begin to redden, I changed the subject. "I found out something interesting a while ago."

"Oh?"

"I can't tell you here. Someone might hear us."

"Do you have any more frozen yogurt?" he asked.

Before I could answer, it happened. Mom spotted Brad and me.

In a flash, she sprung to her feet, and left the three women she was conversing with. Their mouths hung agape as Mom almost broke the hundred-yard-dash record sprinting over to us. "Hi," she said, panting a little. She stuck out her hand. "I'm Helen Smyth, Meg's Mom."

Brad stood up, shook her hand, and said, "Hello, Mrs. Smyth. I'm Brad Trinder." He pulled over a folding chair for her. With bright, bird-like eyes, Mom looked from Brad to me and back.

I sighed. Might as well get it over with. "This is the man I had dinner with the other night."

"Oh, how nice," Mom gushed. "I'm always thrilled to meet Meg's friends."

I knew the routine by now, and if I didn't cut her short, her cross-examination of Brad would push well beyond name, rank, and serial number. "Dad is in Craig's office in the basement. I know Sally would appreciate having them up here mingling with the guests." I gave her a pointed smile, and cut my eyes toward the stairs.

Mom shot me a look that could bring down a ten-point buck. "I'll be right back," she said, as she headed for the basement stairs.

Laughter welled in Brad's eyes. "Nicely played. But really, how bad could your Mom's questions be?"

"Think Inquisition."

§

We decided to move to where Max Trent was in conversation with Pete Winters. Amend that. "Conversation" implies give and take. Max and Pete were speaking monologues in duet. Neither man seemed to listen to what the other was saying.

"Bramble's gotta move with the times," said Max. "No point in staying a one-horse town forever."

"Bramble's a good place to live. Slow pace," said Pete.

"Hi, guys," said Brad. He introduced himself to the others.

"You're working for Porter-Burton, aren't ya?" asked Max. "I saw you with them at the town meeting."

"Well, yes. I'm doing their books," Brad replied.

"With Simon Porter gone, will they change their minds about the Prairie Lake development?" I admired Pete for his forthrightness in asking the question on everyone's mind.

"Well, Simon's death changes the corporate structure. Travis Burton is the head of PBE now. He hasn't mentioned anything about backing out of the development plans."

"Well, he'd better think twice about continuing," Pete said, at the same time Max said, "That's wonderful news."

As Brad and I edged away, leaving Pete and Max to continue their argument, Fred and Frieda Koenig arrived at the gathering. They stopped and surveyed the room. I nudged Brad. "Perhaps they're waiting to be announced."

He grinned and murmured, "Ladies and gentlemen, His Honor the Mayor and his lovely wife."

I nudged him harder. "Shush! They'll hear you." I didn't dare tell him that most of the towns-people referred to the pair as "Freddy Squared," not only because their names were similar, but also because Frieda was known to be the power behind the mayoral throne.

Frieda wore a business suit and sensible shoes. Her frosted hair was teased to a perfect sphere around her head. Her penciled eyebrows gave her hooded eyes a disconcerting look of mild surprise.

The two stepped into the parlor, and began what could only be called "working the room." They split up and circled the room, shaking hands with everyone, inquiring after each person. All that was missing was a baby for Hizzoner to kiss. Frieda reached us first. "Hello there, Meg," she said, shaking my hand. "I hear your parents are in for a visit."

I nodded. "Yes. Short visit. They go back to Arizona tomorrow."

"Well, that will give you more time for your, um, reporting." She gave a little laugh that didn't reach her reptilian eyes. No doubt Fred's brother, Chief Billy, was the source of her remark. I guess it was foolish for me to think I could keep my inquiries on the down-low forever.

She turned to Brad, "So good to see you again, Mr. Trinder. So sorry about what happened to your employer. Between that and the ruckus at the town hall meeting, I'm afraid you're seeing our little town at its worst." She simpered, "I hope we can change your mind about us."

Good grief. I considered reminding Frieda that Brad wasn't a member of the Bramble electorate. No need for her to ooze smarm.

"Thank you, Mrs. Koenig," Brad said. "By the way, are there any new developments in the investigation?"

Frieda's face closed down and she drew herself up. "As the village attorney, I cannot comment on an ongoing investigation."

"Of course not," said Brad.

She moved on to the next group of potential voters.

§

Craig and Dad, with Mom leading the way, emerged from Craig's inner sanctum, and joined Brad and me.

I nodded toward the Koenigs, who were loading up their plates in the dining room. "You missed two Bramble dignitaries, our mayor and his wife."

"Alas," Mom said. "I think the party's on its last legs. I think I am too."

Turning to Craig, I said, "This has been a terrific get-together. Thank you so much. I'll go say good-bye to Sally, see if she needs anything, and then we'll be off."

I found Sally in the kitchen. She had kicked off her shoes and sat on a chair, rubbing her feet. She gave me a tired smile.

"Sally, this was a wonderful party. Everything was just right. Marvelous food. Bramble will be talking about this for years!"

"Thanks, Meg. I hope your parents enjoyed it. Please wish them a safe return to their home."

I gave Sally a hug and returned to the parlor where I had, oh foolish me, left Mom and Dad alone with Brad.

As I approached, Brad was listening atten-
tively to Dad, as he went on about the millwork in
the Montrose home. Mom looked impatient, waiting for Dad to take a breath so she could conduct
an in-depth interview with Brad.

"Time to go," I said.

The four of us walked to the sidewalk,
then to our cars. "I'll be in touch," said Brad to
me. As I drove my parents back to my house, I
thought about what that might mean. Or lead to.

Chapter 22

My parents and I sank into the chairs in my living room. It had been a long day. None of us was hungry, Sally's spread being enough to fend off world hunger for a decade or more.

Mom led off. "Meg, I like your young man."

"Mom, he's not *my* young man. I've had two dates with him. And we're hardly young. Not to mention our last date was a disaster." I went on to tell the story I now thought of as *Folger's and the Feline.* Dad didn't betray that I'd already told him.

"That's terrible, honey," she said. "I wish I'd known. I have a wonderful remedy for—"

Dad interrupted Mom. "Helen, did you learn anything new at the open house?"

"Well, as a matter of fact, I did learn something. I believe I have a nose for news." A nose for news. I didn't know whether to laugh or groan.

"Well, it's the Trents. You know, Max and Claudie," Mom said.

Before Mom could continue, Dad interjected. "That Max is a bag of hot air. All grandiose ideas and no plans to make them a reality."

"I didn't know you talked with Max," I said.

"Oh, yes." Dad cast an apologetic eye at Mom. "Some of the men were with Craig in the basement—"

"Hiding out," I finished his sentence.

"Well, maybe. Anyway, it seems that Max and his wife haven't spoken to each other in months," Dad said. "I didn't ask why."

Mom took back the conversation. "I chatted with Claudie. She told me she's saving up her money so she can leave Max and move to Florida. I didn't much like Claudie. What a snip."

Dad and I exchanged a glance. "Snip" was Mom's substitute word for "bitch."

Mom went on, "I also talked with the funeral director, Winn something. I didn't learn much, other than how much he enjoys his work. He even gave me a brochure. Imagine!" Mom reached for her purse, and drew out a Memory Meadows leaflet, walked over to the wastebasket, and dropped it in. "He's like King Herod."

Dad and I looked at each other. We were used to Mom's *non-sequiturs,* but this baffled us. "Huh?" we asked in unison.

"The New Testament describes Herod as 'clothed in pomposity'." Mom looked at us triumphantly. Dad and I smiled and shrugged.

My parents looked expectantly at me, and I realized I had to keep up my end of the Smyth investigative team's efforts. When Mom volunteered her investigative skills, I made up my mind to save my sanity and not to tell her any more than I had to. Mom had a tendency to weave whole tapestries of information from a few threads. So, I kept mum about Claudie blackmailing Marlene. I seethed inside at the gall of Claudie saying she was saving *her* money, when a lot of it was the Tigrans' money.

"Well, I'm sure that Mayor Koenig is planning to run again for office." I thought a moment, then added, "Or his wife is. They wasted no time in 'pressing flesh' at the open house."

§

Mom made sure we were up in time to attend worship services before driving to the airport. It was another golden autumn day, so we decided to walk to the church. Its bell was pealing as we entered and found places in a pew toward the front, where late arrivers sit. We weren't tardy, according to my mother, unless we followed the choir in as they processed down the aisle—which they did a minute or two later, as Lettie Lansdale, our organist time out of mind, accompanied them in a spritely version of "A Mighty Fortress Is Our God."

Our choir consists of about twenty voices, mostly women. One or two sopranos, most notably Gladys Koenig, felt called to be heroic from time to time, but for the most part, they group sang without creating a high cringe factor. For myself, I love to sing, but am content to make "a joyful noise," my vocal range being out of sync with the keys that hymns seem to be written in.

In the quiet moments during the service, the squeals, giggles, and chatter from the Sunday school could be heard through the wall it shared with the sanctuary. Somehow, I never minded it. Our youth program, under the imaginative leadership of Sandy Wilcox, Babsy's sister, attracted kids of all ages, who, in turn, urged their parents to join Bramble Lutheran. It made for a lively church.

I took a moment or two to enjoy being in this place with my parents on either side of me. I reached over to them, squeezed their hands. Pastor Joe preached on the topic of generosity, which was a lead-in to the church's director of the finance ministry, who talked briefly about the need for immediate funds to shore up the budget. More than the budget needed shoring up. Buckets were placed strategically around the sanctuary today, as rain was expected later.

As we left the church, the warmth of an hour or two ago had disappeared with the sun, and clouds scudded across a lowering sky. Mom and Dad came up behind me, and Pastor Joe turned to shake their hands. I waited at the bottom of the steps for them and we walked back to my house.

§

After returning from O'Hare, where I left my parents at their gate, I got out my note pad and sat down at the kitchen table. My turbulent thoughts spun in a maelstrom. I rested my arms on the table, laid my head on them, and slept.

I awoke to the sound of rain dashing against my windows. It was almost dark. I went through the house and checked all the windows to make sure they were closed. An unblinking Minerva stared at me from the top of the refrigerator. I went to the pantry, noting that Mom hadn't had a chance to rearrange the shelves this visit. Too busy sniffing out mischief with her nose for news. I smiled and I retrieved a can of cat food, and emptied it into a clean dish. Minerva remained where she was.

Although weary to the bone, I managed to add observations and information I gleaned from the Montrose party to my notes. The rain continued thrumming against the panes. A good night to be inside. I trudged up to bed. Glancing out my bedroom window, I glimpsed a light in the empty cottage four doors down. As I watched, the light moved to another window, then disappeared. The house was black again. I stood there for a while, waiting to see if the light reappeared. All was dark. I went to bed.

§

The rain stopped during the night, leaving droplets of water glittering in the grass. The sky was growing light as I dressed and came downstairs. I decided to make a list of something other than murder suspects, clues, and suppositions: chores needing to be done. I put the tablet aside when I remembered the light in the vacant house down the road.

I made a couple of pieces of toast, slathered them with strawberry preserves, and gulped down a cup of coffee. Throwing my old NU sweatshirt over my T-shirt and donning my ratty tennies, I set off down the road. No one was about this early in the morning.

Reaching the vacant house, I squelched across the wet grass to the front door. I knocked. No answer. I tried the knob. To my surprise, it turned, and the door creaked open. The house had been empty a long time, and I hadn't been in it before. The layout was similar to mine, but with an open floor plan. The downstairs was all one room. A huge stone fireplace stood at one end, exuding the damp, charred smell of years of fires.

There was a table and a couple of wobbly chairs at the other end of the room. A settee, its springs broken, sat on the floor nearby. I tried not to disturb any of the myriad spider webs wisping from the ceiling beams. Only a few windowpanes were without cracks. A musty chill permeated the room. I shivered.

So far, there was nothing to indicate anyone had been here. Anyone human, anyway. Mouse droppings dotted the kitchen counters. A partial roll of oilcloth was on one of the counters. The sink was dark with rusty stains and traces of old food.

I turned back to the stairs in the main room. The cold of the rooms was too pervasive to ignore much longer, but I needed to see if the bedrooms upstairs held any clues as to what was going on last night. Along the staircase, great sheets of curling wallpaper hung from the walls like windless sails. I braced myself and started up the stairs.

Chapter 23

The hum and beeping of machines woke me. My mind was out of focus. Faces peered at me as through a fish-eye lens.

"Meg? Meg?" A voice called to me. It seemed so far away.

I wanted to answer. But it was so far away. I drifted…

I woke again. My eyes felt weighted down. I opened them to slits, looked around. Tubes ran from my arms and under the light blankets, where they disappeared. I closed my eyes.

"Meg?" The voice again.

"Uh." I opened my eyes, wider this time. My voice crackled, "Where…?"

"You had a nasty fall, Meg. You're at the hospital. You're going to be okay."

"Alfreda?"

"It's Brad. I'm here."

"Oh." I slept.

§

Nearly two days passed before I was able to stay awake and notice things around me. I pushed aside memories of my last hospital stay after my car was bombed. I was here due to my own stupidity. I determined to remain cheerful. So, the first time a nurse, one of many chipper beings wearing starched caps and white shoes, came in at four in the morning to "take my vitals," I quipped, "How alarming! Are you going to sell them?"

Nurse Chipper was not amused, and launched into a detailed dissertation on pulse, respiration, and blood pressure. I rethought my course of action. If I wanted to leave the hospital before the Cubs won the World Series, I needed to be cheerful and meek. Compliant. No humor. A difficult regimen for me, but I'd be a better person for it. Ugh.

In between pokes and prods designed to advance my recovery, but succeeding only to advance my irritability, I entertained several visitors. "Entertained" is a euphemism. No one is much entertained in a hospital.

Sally came to see me nearly every day. I begged her not to tell my parents what had happened. To no avail. I was thankful Sally told them only that I fell, omitting that I tumbled through a staircase at an empty house. Mom and Dad called twice a day. Mimicking Nurse Chipper's tone, I managed to convince them I had a mild concussion and some bruises, but was not at Death's door.

Sally told me it was Brad who found me at the empty house, after I'd fallen through a rotten step on my way upstairs. I wanted to talk with him, but it wasn't until I was ready to be discharged that he showed up.

"Hi, Meg!" If I have to endure another chipper person, I'll do something desperate. "I'm here to take you home."

"What? I thought Sally or Craig—"

"Nope. Me." My plastic bag of hospital-issued toiletries, medication, instructions, and the like was at the foot of the bed. Nurse Chipper had helped me get dressed, so I was ready. I stood up and would've fallen if Brad hadn't grabbed me.

"You okay?" he asked.

"Yeah. Just have to get my bearings. I've only taken one or two strolls down the corridor with a walker." My weakness passed, and Brad helped me into the obligatory wheelchair to take me outside.

He wheeled me over to a dark blue Oldsmobile sedan. Surprised, I looked at him.

"Motor pool car. Thought it would easier for you than the Porsche."

After I was tucked inside, Brad, keeping the car at least five miles under the speed limit, drove me home. Minerva gave me her best "and where have you been?" look, but relented after Brad had helped me inside and I was seated at the kitchen table. Purring loudly, she jumped into my lap, circled around a couple of times, and curled up.

I asked Brad to stay and tell me what had happened. He hesitated.

"I have frozen yogurt," I coaxed, "unless Sally ate it when she was looking after Minerva."

"Okay, but let me get it out. You stay there," he said. As if I would move with Minerva drowsing on me.

"Mmm. This is divine," I said, my mouth full of yogurt. "There's a limit to how much hospital food a person can stand." I swallowed and said, "Okay, tell all."

"First of all," Brad said, "what on earth were you doing in that vacant cottage?"

"I saw lights inside it the night before."

"So you decided to break in there, all by yourself. What if it was Simon Porter's killer in there?"

I scoffed. "It was daylight. And besides, I didn't break in. I knocked. When I turned the door handle, the door swung open and…"

"And you went right in."

"Well, yeah. I looked around, and I remember starting upstairs…how did you know I was there? I mean, how was it that you found me?"

"Meg, I was the one poking around in there the night before. The light you saw was my flashlight. The power was shut off when the house was abandoned."

"What? Why?"

"I've rented it."

"I don't understand. Rented it for what?"

"To keep an eye on you." He looked at his hands. "Obviously, I didn't do such a good job of it. I never thought you'd go exploring. I only found you as soon as I did—about an hour after you fell, I think—because I brought some groceries and cleaning stuff inside after I arranged to have the power switched on."

"I don't need anyone keeping an eye on me, Brad," I said, annoyed.

"Meg, there's a murderer still on the loose. And you've been asking a lot of questions around town. I don't want anything to happen to you."

I stared at him, my mouth opening and closing like a fish's.

Before I could find my voice, he said, "Now then, it's time for you to get some rest." He walked over, brushed Minerva gently off my lap, picked me up, and carried me upstairs. He paused in the hallway, decided which bedroom was mine, and deposited me inside. "I'll be downstairs if you need anything," he said. "I'll leave the door open, so Minerva won't feel slighted."

I wanted to protest, but the bed beckoned me. I changed into my jammies, climbed in, pulled the covers up, and fell asleep immediately.

§

I woke to the aroma of coffee. Between Mom, and now, Brad, I was getting used to this lifestyle. I grabbed my bathrobe. Mom having seized it and thrown it in the washing machine, there was no cat hair on it. In the bathroom, I took a long look at myself. I had fading bruises on my forearms and forehead. I was a bit stiff from being in bed several days, but other that, I felt pretty good. After a long shower, I put on chinos and a light peach-colored cotton sweater, and started downstairs. Brad must've heard the stairs creak, because he came up to help me.

"Good morning," he said. "You look chipper."

I frowned. "I hope not," I said, telling him about the nickname I'd assigned to my hospital nurse.

He laughed. "Oh, I found some canned cat food, and gave some to Minerva. She gobbled it all up."

"I splurged on that gourmet cat food, but when I feed it to her, she turns up her nose. When you or Mom gives it to her…I'll never understand cats. Someone said that cats have never forgotten they were once worshipped as deities."

Brad laughed. He and I lingered over breakfast. He had whipped up cheese omelets that were wonderful. I was regaining my appetite.

"What are your plans today, Brad?" I asked.

"Well, I'm going to scour out my rental house. I'd better not stay at your house another night. The neighbors will talk."

"Brad, you really don't need to—"

"Stay somewhere else?" He cocked an eyebrow at me.

"Yes, no. I mean, it's silly for you to go to the trouble and expense of renting that house. I can manage fine on my own."

"I have to stay somewhere. And being on the lake is a lot nicer than staying at the hotel."

I changed the subject. "I'd better send some copy to Harry, my editor, so he doesn't think I've been captured by slavers."

He bent down and kissed my forehead. "My phone's hooked up at the house," he said, putting a sheet of paper on the table by the door. "Here're the house and mobile phone numbers. I'm going to run a few errands, but after that, I'm just down the road if you need anything. I'll drop by later, Meg."

Chapter 24

The afternoon sun called to me, so I walked down to the dock. After a few minutes, I decided to take a short walk along the lake. Louis and Jon, my next-door neighbors to the west, lived in the last house on Cottage Row. Next to it was a large wooded area owned by the village. I decided to turn in the opposite direction, and take the foot-path that followed the lake.

The vacant house next door to me on the other side looked forlorn. Weeds were growing in the gutters. I trudged on.

I reached the Fultons' home. I thought about stopping in to say hello, and, I admit, to rest a bit, but Nina and Ben would be at the hardware store now. Reluctant to retrace my steps home, I sat down on a stone bench under one of the two giant spruce trees that stood like sentinels along the path to the Fultons' back door.

Still feeling a bit puny, but determined to make the most of the glorious fall day, I gripped the edge of the bench, pushed myself upright, and continued my walk. I passed the Tigrans' house next door. No signs of life. The children would be at school, Jake working on someone's plumbing, but what would Marlene be doing now that her trysts were at an end? I considered going over there, and thought better of it. She needed some time to think things through.

Kim Winters, wearing lavender scrubs, her curly dark hair tied up in a ponytail, came out on her deck and waved to me as I approached her house. "Come on in, Meg! I've got a bottle of wine that needs tasting."

"Sounds good to me!" I walked over and sat down at the table on her deck.

"What are you doing walking around by yourself?" she asked. "I heard you were in the hospital with a concussion."

"It was nice out…"

"Well, you need to be careful. I don't want to see you in the operating room." Kim was a surgical nurse at Bramble Memorial. "Stay right here. I'll get the wine, and I think I have some cheese and crackers."

I was content to sit.

Kim returned with a bottle of merlot, two Flintstones jelly glasses, and some pretzels. "I guess the boys ate the last of the cheese and crackers, and I always use thick glassware or plastic glasses outside, in case they break. I won't give you too much to drink since you're just getting over a concussion."

"No problem."

After she poured the wine, Kim sat and stretched out her long legs. "Ah. It feels good just to sit. Long shift. Tom and Todd won't be home until late. Football practice."

"The Bramble Bison are off to a good start," I said. The town followed its high-school team faithfully, and the stadium was filled on Friday nights for home games.

"Yep. Three and one. Four games over, four more to go. I worry about the guys getting hurt, but they enjoy it. And as long as they keep their grades up…"

"I saw Pete Saturday at the Montrose open house," I said. "Missed you."

"The nurse who was going to trade shifts with me got sick, so I ended up working both her shift and my own. I'm really sorry I missed the party. I hear Sally and Craig have done wonders with that old house."

"I've been out of touch, being in the hospital," I said. "Have you heard anything about Simon Burton's murder?"

Kim took a sip of her wine. "I don't think there's anything new. Frankly, the whole thing is beyond Billy Koenig's abilities. He's just a small-town cop. Nice enough, but well, not very effective. Or bright."

"I'd have to agree." I munched on a pretzel. "Nothing new on plans for the development?"

"Guess it's going through. I'm sure you know Pete's enraged about it. He's the kind of guy who, when he puts down roots, can't be moved." With a sweep of her hand, Kim drew my eye to the lake, shimmering in the mid-afternoon sun. "This is pretty hard to give up, in any case. I don't know where we could find another place like this, on the lakefront and all—at least, not one we could afford. And the boys are only sophomores. We'd like them to be able to stay and graduate from Bramble High."

I set down my glass. "I'd best be going. Pete will expect dinner, I imagine."

"Who knows when Pete will arrive. Someone in Walnut Creek had a sump pump fail.

He left a message on our answering machine. Something about a crawl space." Kim smiled. "Between Pete and the twins, there's always something swishing around in the washing machine."

The telephone rang. Kim got up. "I'll be right back."

I finished the rest of my glass of wine. Kim was still on the phone. I got up, went over to the door, and stuck my head inside the house to thank Kim and say good-bye. She was sitting on a kitchen stool by the wall phone. Her shoulders shook with sobs.

"Kim! What is it?" I walked over to her.

She looked up, tears streaming down her face. "They've arrested Pete for Simon Porter's murder."

§

Kim ran upstairs and changed her clothes so she could go to the jail. She accepted my offer to stay and wait for her sons to come home from school, grabbed her keys, and bolted out the door. I sat at her kitchen table, and then got up. It was getting dark, so I walked through the downstairs and turned on a couple of lamps. It would be bad enough for the kids to hear that their father was in jail, without having to hear the news in a dimly lit house.

I returned to the kitchen. Dinner. What do strapping teen-age boys eat? An enormous refrigerator, its doors covered with magnets holding notes, football schedules, and other day-to-day trivia of importance, hulked against one wall. I opened it and had my answer: teen-age boys eat a lot. Food filled every shelf. I lifted a corner of aluminum foil from a package: the remains of a beef roast. Rummaging around, I found additional items to warm up for the boys.

It was almost eight o'clock when I heard them come in the back door, and throw their football bags on the laundry-room floor. "Hey, Mom! We're home!"

Two blond giants entered the room. I stood up and went over to them, explaining as best I could that the police had arrested their father. "I'm sure this is all a mistake, and your dad will be home as soon as everything's straightened out." My words sounded insincere to me, maybe because I wasn't sure Pete was innocent. The boys sat down and I served them the food I'd kept warm in the oven.

"When's Mom coming home?" asked Todd. At least, I think it was Todd, but it could've been Tom, as the two were difficult to tell apart.

"I'm not sure. Soon, I think."

The twins sorted their practice uniforms, each piece marked with their team number, and started up the clothes washer. Like flotsam caught in unfamiliar eddies, the boys drifted in and out of the kitchen.

It was nearly ten when Kim came in. Although only a few hours had passed since I last saw her, her face was drawn and ashen

"Thank you so much, Meg, for being here."

"What happened?" We all asked at once.

"He's not actually arrested, Chief Koenig said. The police brought him in for questioning. He'll be held at the Bramble lock-up overnight. Unless they officially charge him. Then he'll be moved to the county jail in Walnut Creek."

Todd and Tom went over to Kim and wrapped their arms around her, and the three stood together, swaying in a hug.

It was time for me to go home. I turned to leave.

"Wait, Meg," Kim said. "Tom or Todd will walk you home."

"No, no. You all should be together, help each other get through this."

Kim didn't press the point. "Well, at least take this with you." She handed me a large flashlight. "Be careful."

"Good luck," I said. "I'm sure things will be sorted out and Pete will be home in no time." I walked outside, and I turned on the flashlight. Unlike those in my junk drawer at home, this one worked.

§

My progress home was snail-like. I was exhausted, my head throbbed, and I had to be careful not to stumble on the uneven dirt path. The light from the flashlight arced only a few feet ahead of me, so I kept my eyes on the ground. The breeze of the afternoon had chilled into a cold wind. I hunched my shoulders against its icy fingers. There were no lights in the Tigran and Fulton homes; their occupants were probably cozied up in their beds by now. Trees, their gnarled arms black against the dark sky slashed by a scimitar moon, threw restless shadows across my path. I heard something behind me and looked back over my shoulder. A formless shape loomed in the darkness. I quickened my step. Footsteps drew closer. I began to run.

Chapter 25

Hands grabbed me and spun me around. A voice rasped, "What the hell do you think you're doing?"

I gasped. The face a few inches from mine was only partially illuminated by my flashlight. I was terrified. My heart pounded in my ears. As I tried to pull free, my flashlight fell to the ground with a thud. I tried to scream, but no sound came out.

"Meg! It's me, Brad."

My knees gave way and I would've collapsed if he hadn't held on to me. He held me for a long minute until I could stand on my own. He took off his windbreaker, and draped across my shoulders.

"I-I…you scared me." My voice shook.

"What are you doing out here at night by yourself? The Montroses and I have been frantic."

"Wh-what?"

"I came by around dinner time, and you were gone. Your door was unlocked, the house was dark, and Minerva hadn't been fed. When you didn't return, I called Sally. She hadn't heard from you either. Where have you been?"

Before I could answer, we reached my house, its lights cheerful in the inky darkness. Brad settled me on the couch and covered me with the afghan I kept there. Minerva appeared from nowhere, as was her custom, kneaded the afghan, and curled up on my chest. Brad opened the fireplace damper and lit the fire that was already laid. Leaving Minerva and me, he went to the kitchen. I could hear him talking with Sally on the phone, reassuring her that I was okay. He returned with two mugs. "Hot chocolate," he said, "with a bit of brandy." I took the mug he handed me, and cradled it in both hands, enjoying its warmth.

"Drink some of that," Brad said. "And then we're going to have a nice long talk."

I obeyed. After a while, I started, "I didn't intend to be out more than an hour."

"You left your door unlocked."

"We do that in Bramble."

He gave me an incredulous look. "Meg, there's been a homicide in Bramble."

Ignoring him, I continued, "I sat on the dock for a while. I felt fine, so I went for a walk and Kim Winters invited me in for a glass of wine and a chin-wag."

"Chin-wag?"

"My mother grew up on a farm a few miles outside Topeka. 'Chin-wag' is one of what she calls her 'Kansas expressions.' It means—"

"I get what it means." Brad was impatient.

"You needn't be cross."

"Needn't be cross after all the worry you've caused?" He shook his head, and in a gentle voice said, "Okay, okay. Go on."

"While I was there, she got a phone call. Pete's been taken into custody." In an odd way, I was pleased to note that Brad was surprised by the news.

"Kim left for the police station, while I stayed at her house. When the twins got home from football practice, I fixed them something to eat, and waited until Kim returned a little after ten. She offered to have one of the boys walk me home, but—"

"But Ms. Independent declined assistance."

"That's not fair!" I sat up, dislodging the cat. "I thought the boys should stay home with their mother."

Brad raised his hands in mock defeat. "I yield. Listen, neither of us has eaten all day. Stay here by the fire. I'll see what I can find in your kitchen."

I stared into the flames and must've dozed a little, because Brad's voice as he returned startled me. "Here we are, another Trinder omelet for your enjoyment."

I smiled. "Thanks, Brad. I really appreciate this—and you."

We ate in silence. Brad said, "I'm going to call the police station in the morning and see what I can find out about Pete Winters."

"He had a gun like the one used to kill Simon Burton." I said. "It was stolen from Pete's truck."

Brad looked astonished. "How do you know that?"

"Pete told me."

"I have a feeling you know a lot more about all this, don't you?"

I grinned. "Maybe."

Brad looked at his watch. "It's nearly midnight. You are going to bed," he said. "And tomorrow we're going to have a, um, chin-wag."

He banked the fire, and carried me upstairs once again, waited for me to change clothes
in the bathroom, and get into bed. "Call me when
you wake up—or if you need anything." He kissed
my forehead. Brad's footsteps faded as he went
downstairs.

I could get used to having him tuck me
in…

§

There was a rap on my back door the next morning as I was emptying the dishwasher. I looked out
the kitchen window, and saw Sally standing on the
porch.

"Hi," I said as I let her in. "Coffee?"

"Don't you 'coffee' me, Meg Smyth! We
were worried sick about you. You've only been
out of the hospital a day or so. We thought maybe
you had a dizzy spell, had fallen—"

"I'm sorry. I went out for a short walk and
it turned into something more. Please sit." I told
her about Pete Winters. As I finished, Brad came
in.

"I didn't hear you knock," I said.

"You door was unlocked. As usual," he
replied as he pulled up a chair. How can he be so

kind and considerate last night, and so snarky this morning. I screwed up my face and gave him the stink eye. It went unnoticed, except by Sally, who gave me a questioning glance.

The coffee pot contained only black sludge, so I set out three glasses, and brought a pitcher of iced tea over to the table from the refrigerator.

Sally said, "I think we need to debrief."

Brad looked puzzled.

"You know, from our party. Things we found out." Sally turned to Brad. "Meg and I were going to compare notes on Monday, but then Meg ended up in the hospital." Sally paused. "But this is better. Brad can lend his expert opinion."

I said nothing as I gathered my notes from under my laptop and gave the other two pencils and paper.

"Before we talk about the people at the party," Brad said, " I talked to Chief Koenig this morning about Pete Winters. Is Billy Koenig always so thick? Never mind. Rhetorical question." Brad continued, "Pete never reported his Glock stolen. The murder weapon hasn't been found, so the police don't know whether Pete's is the gun used to kill Porter. They found the shell casing, but couldn't get any prints from it. It's to Pete's credit that he volunteered the information that he owned one. He said he bought it at a gun show for home protection, but Kim wouldn't have it in the house, so he kept it in the truck."

"But why did the Chief bring in Pete?" Sally asked. "Because he was spear-heading the protest about the Prairie Lake plan?"

"That was part of it," said Brad. "That, and the fact he had no alibi for the time of the shooting."

"But he must have!" I said. "Simon was shot sometime after the town hall meeting, which was a Friday. In fact, the meeting started early so people could go to the Bison game. Pete was at his sons' football game. He never misses one."

"Not this time. Something went wrong with the power at the stadium. No lights, no game. Pete says he was home that night, but his wife was working, and his two boys were at the coach's house for most of the evening."

Sally said, "So Pete admitted to having a gun, which hasn't been found. He was against the development. And he was home alone. That's it? Pretty flimsy."

"No one thinks about needing an alibi when they're home by themselves," I said.

"Yeah. I think ol' Billy Koenig thought he'd break Pete, that Pete would confess and ask for a deal, just like on TV," Brad said. "Sanity, in the form of Pete's lawyer, prevailed. Pete was released a little while ago."

We moved on to discuss the Montrose open house. "My mother decided to play detective at your party."

"What!" exclaimed Sally and Brad.

"I know, I know. Believe me, I know. Dad got into the act, too. Anyway, before my folks went back to Arizona on Sunday afternoon, we shared tidbits we picked up. Between them, my parents learned that Max and Claudie haven't spoken to each other in months, Max thinks Claudie's having an affair, and Claudie's saving up her money to leave Max and move to Florida. And I found out that Marlene Tigran and Simon were having an affair, and Claudie's been blackmailing Marlene over it."

Recalling the venomous remarks I overheard Claudie make to Marlene in the music room, I added, "I wonder if Claudie was jealous of the pair, maybe wanted Porter to herself, have him whisk her away to Florida. When Sally and I were at the motel talking with Claudie, I saw a book with Marlene's name written it. So I went back to the motel, supposedly to take a paperback to Claudie, and asked a few more questions. I saw a gun in a drawer behind the counter in the motel office."

"And those wilted flowers at Marlene's were like the ones in front of the cabin," said Sally.

"Good point," I replied. "I hadn't thought of that."

I cast a sidelong glance at Brad. As I suspected, talking in woman-to-woman shorthand, as long-time friends do, Sally and I left him in the dust.

Sally said, "Simon is a *persona non grata* as far as Jon is concerned. Simon told Jon that Louis was involved with, or hoping to be involved with, some young man staying at the hotel. I advised him to talk with Jon before—"

"Before they go to Denmark this winter for a civil union," I finished. "I overheard some of your conversation with Jon the other day, Sally."

"Why didn't you say so?" asked Sally, a spark of irritation in her eyes.

"I didn't have a chance. You were in your Madam Sally mode." Oh, please, oh please, drop it, Sally.

Sally's mouth twitched as mischief replaced her irritation. "Ah yes. All is forgiven."

"Then there's Freddy Squared." I quickly changed the subject before she could reprise her Madam Sally prognostication.

Brad looked nonplussed. "Stop, you two! You're driving me crazy. Madam Sally, Max, Claudie, Marlene, Denmark. I am completely at sea. And what in the world is 'Freddy Squared'?"

"Who, not what," I said. "Freddy Squared is what Mayor Koenig and his wife are called— behind their backs, of course. His name's Frederick, hers is Frieda. Mom pointed out that the Prairie Lake development might have an impact on the next Bramble mayoral election, even though it's not for a couple of years. The way

Freddy Squared were working the room, I'm sure they're aware of that."

"I must be on my way," Sally said. "Craig and I are going to try that new Italian place over in Walnut Creek. Maybe take in a movie."

"What movie?"

"After a sophisticated compromise involving 'rock, paper, scissors,' Craig and I are seeing *The Mask of Zorro.*"

"Out of the night, when the full moon is bright, comes a horseman known as Zorro…" I sang, as Sally drove away. My version of whistling in the dark. I couldn't avoid talking with Brad any more.

I walked inside where Brad was waiting.

Chapter 26

I busied myself feeding Minerva. As I reached across the table to remove the iced-tea glasses, Brad caught my wrist. "Meg, it's time we talked."

I sat down opposite him and waited. Over the past few days, I could not help be aware of the growing tension between us. I could tell he felt it too. Our carefree architectural tour down the Chicago River seemed eons ago.

"I'll start," he said. "Who's Alfreda?"

"Alfreda?" I stalled. His question was unexpected. There weren't many days when I didn't think about her. I was reluctant to go through it all again, yet I knew he was right. We couldn't go on with so much unsaid.

"You called her name several times in the hospital as you came out of the anesthesia."

"The hospital," I said, "brought back memories I'd hoped to forget."

Brad was quiet, his eyes on mine.

Haltingly, I told him about the Deep Tunnel story, the bomb, and Alfreda's death. "We were all so cocky, all set to win Pulitzers..." I couldn't go on. I felt tears course down my cheeks. Brad grabbed a handful of paper napkins and handed them to me.

"Meg," he said, "Please, don't tell me if you don't want to. I'm so sorry."

"I want to tell you. I'll be okay. Just give me a minute." The room was quiet; the only sound was the wall clock ticking away the passage of time. "Not much more to tell. After I recovered, Harry Josten—my editor—was great, gave me all the time I needed, but I couldn't go back to investigative reporting. The Miss Polly column was, is, a godsend. I love to write.

"You know what the worst thing is, Brad? The Deep Tunnel construction continues, and so does the graft and corruption. We identified a problem without coming up with a solution. And for what?"

Brad came around in back of my chair, and massaged my shoulders. "But it's in your DNA, isn't, Meg? Reporting, I mean. That's why you're looking into the Porter homicide."

I reached over my shoulder and grabbed one of his warm hands. "Oh, Brad, maybe, I don't know anymore. I felt like a quitter, that the bastards, whoever they were, drove me out of

Chicago, out of my career. And yet, I love it here in Bramble."

"You've found out a lot, Meg, but, by now, everyone in town knows you're trying to track down the killer. It's dangerous."

"I promised Harry—"

"That you'd do this no matter what the risk?"

"Well, no," I said, "he was concerned. About my emotional health, I guess you'd say."

"He sounds like a smart and caring guy. Maybe you should consider…"

"I can't quit again, Brad. That I know."

"You're the most stubborn woman I've ever met, Meg." Brad sighed. "Tell you what. Why don't we work on this together? I can't do much, officially, as far as investigating a local homicide, but perhaps I can look into things, unofficially."

I turned in my chair and looked up at him. "You'd do that?"

Brad sighed again. "I know you're going to continue poking around whether I assist you or not. If I help you, I have a better chance of keeping you from getting hurt."

Chapter 27

Brad gave my shoulders a squeeze. "Will you be okay, Meg?" he asked.

"Sure," I answered. "Actually, it feels good to have talked to you about things."

"I wish I could stay longer, but I have an appointment with Jim Dowd, the county coroner, at his office. Simon Porter's remains have been released, and Edwin and Susanne asked me to attend to the details for transporting Simon's remains to Chicago."

"Oh, did the Porters go back to Chicago?"

"Not yet," Brad said. "They and Travis Burton plan to return sometime tomorrow."

After Brad drove off, I went upstairs to splash cold water on my face. The mirror returned a verdict of puffy and red-rimmed eyes. I wet a rag, wrung it out, and went into the bedroom. A few minutes lying down with the cool, damp rag over my eyes turned out to be over two hours.

§

I felt muzzy after sleeping away part of the day. Downstairs, I poured a glass of orange juice and brought it into the living room where Minerva crouched on the arm of the sofa. I sat down and scratched her chin while her eyes closed in rapture. Shaking off thoughts about Brad, the murder, and his offer of help, I downed the juice. "Sorry, girlfriend," I said to her. "Gotta get some work done around here."

With the shortness of my parents' visit and his emphysema, Dad didn't mow the grass as usual, so the grass was long and going to seed. After the rain the other day, I would soon need a machete to trim it.

Blinking in the afternoon sun, I went over to the shed, wheeled out the mower, and plugged in the cord. After wrenching my shoulder the year before pulling the cord to start my gasoline-driven lawn mower, I bought an electric one. Despite dire thoughts of electrocution, I haven't even come close to running over the thick, orange power cord. The grass was longer than I thought, so it was about an hour before I finished up. As I coiled the cable, Louis Briggs came up to me. Dressed in a sport shirt and slacks, with a sweater arranged casually around his neck, he looked like an ad from *GQ*.

"Hi, Meg," he said. "You look like you could use a cold drink about now. We've been at the restaurant all morning, putting things together for the hotel's happy hour. Thought we'd take a break before going back to the Heron for the dinner crowd. Come on over. Jon's fixed his famous raspberry iced tea." Louis grinned and said, "Well, it would be famous if anyone knew about it."

"Oh, Louis, I'm so grungy."

"Nonsense. We're out on our patio." I looked over to see Jon at their table, waving at me and pointing to an empty chair under their green and yellow patio umbrella.

"You've made me an offer I can't refuse," I said.

Jon, in jeans and a light-blue sweater pushed up to his elbows, rose from his seat. "Hi, Meg. It's been ages since I've seen you. I know you've been to the Heron a few times, but Louis keeps me manacled to the kitchen stove." The two men smiled at each other. Jon poured a large glass of iced tea, making sure some of the raspberries floating in it made it into my glass. He handed me a straw. "Helps keep the raspberries from running down your face while you're sipping."

"Mm, this is wonderful," I said. The straw kept me from draining the tea at one gulp. I looked up at the umbrella. "Green and yellow? And that logo? Tell me you're not Green Bay Packers fans."

"It's green and *gold*," said Jon. "Go Pack!"

"Uh-oh. I can't believe I've lived here all this time and didn't know this. Now, I'm fraternizing with the enemy," I said, "Bear down, Chicago Bears!"

"Who's coaching the Bears this year?" Louis asked with a grin.

"Very funny. Dave Wannstadt is still with us—probably not for long, the way the season's going."

"Aww," Louis and Jon said in unison.

We talked a while about the Cubs, who had a winning record for a change, and Sammy Sosa's home runs. I remembered being surprised, when I first met Louis and Jon, that they were into sports. Another gay stereotype shattered.

"Your house looks great," I said, leaning back and looking up at it. The two men had gutted the inside of their cottage, added on several square feet of living space, and transformed it into what was, arguably, the loveliest home in Cottage Row.

The landscaping was exquisite, with something always in bloom. Even in winter, red berries winked out from the evergreens.

"Thanks, Meg. It was mostly Louis's idea," said Jon. "He has a great eye." Louis reached over and squeezed Jon's hand. It appeared all was well between them.

"Okay, Meg. We've plied you with drink, albeit non-alcoholic. Time to tell all," said Louis.

"All? About what?"

"My dear girl, we live next door, remember? We've seen that hunky man visiting you," said Jon.

"At all hours," added Louis. "I even saw him leaving your house one morning."

"Nothing is sacred in this town," I replied. I felt my face grow warm, and hoped it wouldn't be noticed with my face flushed from mowing the grass in the sun.

"Just looking after our neighbor," said Jon. "Well? We're waiting with bated breath."

"His name is Brad Trinder. He does accounting—"

Louis and Jon hooted. "Is that what they call it now?" Jon said.

"—for Porter-Burton Enterprises," I said.

"We'll try not to hold that against him," said Jon, "although PBE isn't exactly high on our list."

"So you're against the development?" I asked.

"We certainly are," said Jon. "We love it here. We have a business we enjoy and a house we adore. And the people are best of all. Bramble folks, at least most of them, are tolerant of our relationship."

"The police don't seem to be making much progress on Simon Porter's murder."

"No," said Louis. "And no one seems to be mourning him. He tried to break us up by telling Jon untrue stories about me."

"Why would Simon want to do that?" I asked.

"Maybe he thought we'd sell to him if we weren't together. Or maybe he was just a garden variety homophobe."

"Yeah, maybe he thought we were contagious," said Jon.

"Enough about Simon the Scumbag, said Louis. "You will have us do your engagement party, right? We could do it all in green and gold."

I had to laugh. "You guys are too much. Brad and I had two dates. Two. That's all."

"And was that not your Brad I saw carrying things into the empty house down the way?" asked Louis.

"You're as bad as my mother. He's not *my* Brad. Nothing gets by you. How do you see these things, living here at the end of Cottage Row?"

"Answer Louis's question, Missy," said Jon, "or no more raspberry iced tea for you."

"Yes, he's renting the house for a while, rather than staying at the Prairie Palace Hotel, while he works with PBE's development project."

Jon refilled my glass, and we talked a bit longer before I thanked them and started across their lawn to my house. Jon caught up to me and grabbed my hand. "Meg, seriously, if you ever need any help, please call on us."

§

After I put away the mower, I watched the ducks swimming close to the shore. Once in a while, they'd bob for food, their heads in the water, and feet in the air. The golden hour just as the sun set, so prized by photographers, bathed the lake in shimmers of gold. A small flock of Canada geese flew by, practicing their V-formation for their long flight south. I wished them well, safe from hunters on their journey.

I went inside, grateful Brad hadn't been by to notice that I hadn't locked my back door.

I cleaned up and decided to take the kayak out. The weather forecast was for one of those twenty-degree drops in temperature over the next few days, so there may not be many more days like this. As I paddled, I thought about Brad. I still didn't know who he was, really. He had no real home, he was divorced, and he was an FBI agent. Craig Montrose vouched for him, but I wondered how much he really knew about Brad Trinder. My thoughts alternated between scolding myself for being too suspicious, and being so naïve to trust a man I'd only known for a short while. I steered the boat toward home, and pulled it up on the shore and turned it over to keep the rain out. I needed to settle this. I telephoned Sally and invited myself over. I had to talk with Craig.

§

Sally greeted me with a hug. "This is a such a nice surprise, Meg. Come on in. Can I get you something?"

"No, I'm fine. Actually, I've come over to talk to Craig."

"Craig?"

"I need to know more about Brad."

"Things getting more serious with him, aren't they?" asked Sally. "Don't look shocked. He was at the hospital almost every time I was there to see you. How do you feel about Brad?"

"I don't honestly know, Sally. There's been no, you know—"

"Hanky-panky?" finished Sally with a grin.

"You're incorrigible," I said. "Anyway, I hate to not trust Brad, but on the other hand…"

"Has he told you anything about himself?" asked Sally.

"Not much," I said, "and I hate to look like I'm pumping him for information, or conducting an interview, or checking up, or…"

"I understand. Craig's in the cave. Why don't you go down there and talk things over with him?"

Sally walked me to the stairs leading to the lower level and called down, "Craig? Meg is here to see you."

"I'll come upstairs, Sally. I have a feeling I know what she wants," came Craig's voice.

Craig gave me a hug, and the three of us went into the parlor. The Montroses sat on a loveseat opposite my chair.

"Did you want me to stay, Meg?" Sally asked.

"Of course. Did you know Brad before he came to Bramble?"

"Not personally, just from Craig mentioning him."

"Craig, there's no way to ask this, so I'll plunge in. What can you tell me about Brad Trinder?"

"I've known Brad for several years. We've worked together tracing laundered money and suspicious activity. He's a brilliant forensics accountant. He's been with the Bureau for almost fifteen years, I think."

"What's he like?" I asked.

"Pretty much, what you see is what you get. He's a good guy." Craig paused. "You know he's been married?"

"Yes, he told me that he's divorced, that they lived in Maryland."

"Did he say anything else about it?"

"N-no, not really. Why? What happened?"

Craig thought for a moment, and said, "Meg, I don't feel comfortable telling you the details. It was a difficult time for Brad, and you're the first woman he's shown any interest in since he and his wife parted ways. You're good for him. You're fun, intelligent, and down-to-earth. When the time is right, I'm sure he'll tell you."

§

I drove home, put my purse and keys on the hall table, and decided I didn't know much more than before. I smiled to myself. He wasn't a serial killer, at least, but Brad Trinder was still a mystery man.

Chapter 28

Quiet. It seemed a long time since I had the house to myself. I'm rarely bored in my own company, and this evening was no exception. I put a load of dirty clothes in the washing machine and ran a mop over the kitchen floor. I took a quick inventory of food I had on hand, and put together a chicken casserole.

While it baked in the oven, I booted up my laptop and started a Miss Polly article. The supply of advance columns I sent Harry was almost depleted. I tapped away on the keyboard, pausing once in a while to think and sip a glass of wine I'd poured for myself.

I had just finished my writing, and was looking over what I had so far, when there was a knock at the door, followed by someone rattling the knob. I looked out. It was Brad. I'd remembered to lock the door when I came back from the Montrose house, so for once, I wouldn't receive a lecture from him.

"Hi, Brad, come on in," I said, as I opened the door.

He glanced at the kitchen table. "Am I interrupting your work? I should've called, I guess," he said.

"No problem. Come in, come in. Have some wine?"

"No thanks. Just thought I'd check up on you." Seeing my look, he said, "I know, I know. Glad to see your door was locked. I didn't get back until now. Turns out, the Porters met with their attorney to straighten out probate issues at the county courthouse. He drove them back to the hotel here, while I went into Chicago and followed up with the funeral-home arrangements at that end."

"Why did you have to do that? Shouldn't Edwin and Susanne do those things tomorrow or today when they were finished with their attorney?" I bit my tongue. I sounded shrewish and possessive. It was none of my business and, as I keep telling people, he's not *my* Brad.

Before Brad could answer, the phone rang. I motioned for Brad to sit down while I answered it.

"Hello?"

"Meg! I'm so glad you're there." It was Kim Winters. "I'm here at the hospital."

"What happened?" Out of the corner of my eye, I saw Brad look up.

"Gita Banicki. She's here. Another heart attack," said Kim.

"Another—?"

"She's been here twice before and pulled through. She's in a coma."

"When did it happen?" I asked.

"Late morning or early afternoon. She came in by ambulance."

"How is Tony taking it?"

"I saw him earlier. He's devastated, of course. I think he may have gone home for a bit to get some things for his mother, although I don't think—"

"I'll go over to their house and see if I can be of help."

"Oh, would you? That would be great. I'm on shift here for another couple of hours."

"Thanks for letting me know, Kim." I hung up just as the oven timer went off. I took the casserole out, and set it on top of the stove.

"That was Kim Winters," I said to Brad. "Gita Banicki, Tony's mother, is in the hospital. She had a heart attack. Kim didn't sound very hopeful about her recovery. She's in a coma. I think I'll take this casserole over to Tony while it's still warm."

"What is it with women and casseroles in times of troubles?" Brad said. "I'll walk you over."

There was a light on inside the Banicki house. Tony answered our knock.

"Hi, Tony. I am so sorry to hear about your mother," I said. "You know Brad?

Tony and Brad shook hands. "Yes, we met at the Montrose party," said Tony. "Won't you both come in?"

"For a minute," I said. Brad and I stepped into the living room. "I brought you something to eat when you have a chance. Just heat it up in your oven." As I handed the casserole to Tony, the lid clattered to the floor.

"Oh, Tony, I'm so sorry. I should've taped down that cover." I picked it up, put it back on the dish, and handed it to him again. "I'm afraid some of the casserole spilled on your lovely wood floor.

Do you have a rag? Point me toward your kitchen and I'll get a rag."

"No! I mean, please don't bother. I'll get one," he said. Tony left the room and reappeared with a wet rag. He bent down and took a couple of swipes at the floor with the cloth.

"How is your mother?" Brad asked.

"Not good, I'm afraid," said Tony. "I came back for her Bible. It's in Polish. She's in a coma, so I don't know if she can hear me or not, but I thought she might…" His voice trailed off.

"We should go, Tony," I said, "let you get back to the hospital."

"Actually, I was on my way there." Tony said as he grabbed both sets of keys on the hall table, thrust one set in his pocket, and locked the door. The three of us stood for a moment outside. "Thanks again, Meg, Brad. This is so kind of you."

Tony got into his car and drove off. Brad walked me back home, gave me a peck on the cheek, saw me in, and walked toward his house.

§

I sat down at my kitchen table and absently stroked Minerva, who had bounded into my lap. I must've missed hearing the ambulance this afternoon when I was sleeping. In my mind, I went over the occupants of the other Cottage Row houses. During the week, almost everyone was at work during the day. Louis and Jon were at the restaurant until mid-afternoon, so they wouldn't have heard the ambulance either. How sad that Tony had no one to call, to be with him at this unhappy time.

I turned off the lights, checked the locks, and headed for bed, Minerva dashing up the stairs in front of me. Weary though I was, something nagged at me, something I missed. The more I tried to grasp it, the more elusive it became. I fell into a fitful sleep.

Sometime later, I woke. The room was chilly. As predicted, the temperature had dropped, and my bedroom window overlooking the lake was open. I went over and closed it. I was halfway back to bed when I went back to the window again. My kayak was gone. I probably hadn't pulled it far enough on shore this afternoon. I shrugged my shoulders. Too late to do anything about it now. I pulled up the covers to my chin,

Minerva wrapped herself around my head, and we burrowed down for the rest of the night.

Chapter 29

A fresh day, and I finally felt like my normal self. The slight headache from my concussion was gone. Funny how I didn't realize I had a headache until it was no more.

Minerva sat at the kitchen window, making that strange noise in her throat designed to lure an unsuspecting bird. I looked outside and saw a pair of cardinals in the bush outside the window, safe from my house cat. I also noticed my kayak, its paddle lying across the seat, was back on the shore. Did I imagine it was gone last night? Perhaps a trick of shadows caused by the moon behind the clouds? The boat had my name and registration sticker on it. A kind person must've found it and brought it ashore.

I was back at the computer when someone from Cottage Row knocked at the back door. People living on Cottage Row always took the path to one another's door. Only villagers and strangers came to the front door.

"Hi," I said, as I opened the door to Brad. "You're up early. What's up?"

"Meg, I wanted to tell you myself." He paused. "Edwin Porter was killed. They found him early this morning."

"Oh, no! Where? When?" I asked.

"Travis called me. Edwin's body was found just outside the construction yard. "

As I grabbed my jacket off the hook by the door, and shrugged into it, Brad blocked my exit.

"Brad, I've got to get out there," I said, trying to push my way past him.

"Hold on, Meg," he said. "I know you have to report it for the *Journal*. But slow down. No one else, other than the official people, knows about it yet. I'll drive you there and fill you in on the way.

"A passing motorist noticed Edwin's car parked in front of the yard. It was about four in the morning," Brad began.

"Edwin's car?" I asked.

"That big Lincoln PBE rented. They kept it to use while they were here."

"Oh, that's right. Sorry. Go on," I said.

"The guy thought it was odd that such an expensive car was at the yard, especially at that hour, so he got out and walked around the car. The car was locked. He found Edwin propped up in front of the gate to the yard."

"Not posed in a backhoe?" I asked.

"No. The gates have been locked since Simon's death, so the killer had to settle for this, I guess. The coroner put the time of death twelve to sixteen hours before he was found. No murder weapon left behind, but the lake's nearby."

"Was Edwin shot too?"

"No, he'd been bludgeoned. His head was…" Brad paused, "uh, a mess."

§

We pulled up to the yard and walked up to the gate, which was now open. A coroner's van, its doors open, showing the racks of instruments, tools, and equipment inside, was parked in the yard. A man and a woman, wearing dark brown jackets with "Seminole County" lettered in beige on the backs, were methodically searching the grounds. Brad walked over to them, showed his badge, and talked with them for a few minutes.

As I waited for him to return, I stayed where I was, not wanting to disturb the crime scene.

I groaned. Picking his way toward me through the mud was Chief Billy Koenig. I suppressed a grin when he stepped in a puddle only slightly less deep than Lake Ontario. He slogged on toward me.

"Hi, Meg. How's the little journalist today?"

I clenched my fists until my finger nails bit into my palms. Billy, with that condescending remark, you are so close to becoming the third victim. Aloud, I asked, "What can you tell me, Chief?"

Brad came up to us, as Billy replied, "Looks like an assault." I couldn't meet Brad's eyes. I knew, without looking, his eyeballs were rotating nearly fast enough to break the sound barrier.

"Hello, Chief," Brad said, showing great composure. "They haven't found much blood, so I guess it's likely Edwin was killed somewhere else and brought here."

"Yep, that's what I thought, too," said Billy. He walked away.

"How does that man keep his job?" Brad asked me.

"He serves at the pleasure of his brother, the mayor."

Before Brad and I left, I took photographs of the van and the coroner's people scouring the area, avoiding Billy Koenig's ploys to inveigle his way into the photos. Brad dropped me off at home so I could e-mail my story to Harry at the *Journal-Times.*

Harry called as soon as he received it. "Wow, Meg, looks as if you've stumbled into quite a situation. Promise me you'll stay safe. I can send someone else out there—"

"I'm fine, Harry. Please don't worry." I was touched at his concern, but after all my work, I didn't want another *Journal* reporter to come here from Chicago and take over my story. "Off the record," I added, "there's an FBI agent here who's taken a bit of unofficial interest."

"That's good to know. Okay, Meg, but please holler if—"

"I will, Harry."

§

Brad dropped by a little later. "I'm on my way to Fulton's Hardware. I've got to patch the roof on the house before it rains," he said, "but I wonder if you'd like to go to the hotel with me later?" He flashed me that devilish look of his. "For happy hour, that is."

"Sounds good to me." I gave him a roguish smile. "For happy hour, that is."

After he left, Minerva bounded to the top of the refrigerator as I jumped up and down, pumping my fist. "Yes!"

After I took a shower and washed my hair, I went to the closet for something to wear, sliding the clothes hangers back and forth several times. Good grief, woman. Make a choice. The guy's seen you in the hospital, at your worst, for heaven's sake, and he's still interested. I pulled on a pair of slacks and a sweater, and went downstairs to wait.

I glanced out the kitchen window and saw Brad limping down the path to my house. I hurried out and assisted him inside. "What happened to you?" I asked.

"Damn roof was slippery," he said. "I lost my balance."

"Brad! Are you okay? Did you fall off?"

"Not quite. My ankle got twisted in the gutter. It stopped me from falling, but my ankle's not in great shape." He hobbled over to the table and sat down in a chair.

"Let's see it," I said.

"It's okay, honest," he said.

I gave him The Look, perfected by generations of Rasmussen women and handed down to me from Mom.

He pulled up his trouser leg. His ankle ballooned over his shoe.

"We're going to the Emergency Room and have that looked at," I said.

"No, really, it'll be okay."

Brad soon realized there is no arguing with The Look. He handed his gun to me. "You'd better hold on to this. They'll probably take X-rays, and it would be difficult to explain."

I gingerly put the weapon in my purse and helped him into my car. We sped off to Bramble Hospital.

§

Television programs portray ERs as exciting, with life-and-death decisions made every moment. Perhaps this is true behind the curtains, but in the waiting room, it's hurry up and wait. We hurried in, waited in line to fill out forms, hurried to find two chairs together, and waited for Brad's name to be called. Finally, he was wheeled off to have his ankle X-rayed.

After a while, I stood in line again, and asked if I could check on another patient while I was here. The woman on duty behind the desk said in a sotto voice, "Yes, but you really should go to the main admissions desk. I need to keep the phone lines open."

"I only want to see if my friend is still here. Gita Banicki."

"I'll check. Just a moment." She consulted a list. "Yes, she's in Intensive Care. Room 407."

"Thank you so much," I said. I returned to my seat. I couldn't visit her now, but at least I knew Gita was still alive.

An attendant carrying a pair of crutches wheeled Brad into the waiting room. His foot, encased in a rigid splint, was thrust out in front of the wheelchair. Before I could ask, Brad said, "They couldn't find even a hairline fracture, so they're treating it as a bad sprain. I need a little practice with these crutches, and I'll be fine."

He handed me two slips of paper. "If we could stop at the drug store and get these prescriptions filled before you take me back to my house, that would be great."

"What do you mean 'take you back to your house'? Are you crazy? You're coming home with me."

"No, I can't impose on you. And what will the neighbors think? Your reputation will be ruined."

"First of all, it's not an imposition. You make wonderful omelets. Secondly, it's too late about the neighbors. Jon and Louis already have, shall we say, drawn conclusions from your visits. Besides, it might be fun to have a certain reputation," I said, giving him a devilish smile.

"Yeah, but I feel like *The Man Who Came to Dinner*."

"Except I've never fed you dinner," I replied, wondering how he felt about peanut butter and banana sandwiches.

The hospital orderly and I managed to get Brad inside my little car, once we rolled down the passenger-side window so the crutches could stick out of it. I drove straight home, and called in the prescriptions. Bramble's pharmacy still makes home deliveries. While I waited, I made up a bed for Brad on the couch and handed him the television remote. I placed his gun among the magazines on the table nearby. The delivery boy arrived about a half-hour later. I gave Brad a couple of pills and saw his eyelids grow heavy. I covered him up, turned out the light, and went upstairs to bed.

I was about to drop off to sleep, when I bolted upright. My parents! A second murder would surely be picked up by the Phoenix news media. I had to call them and set their minds at ease before they read about it, or they'd be on the first flight out. I laughed aloud. It might almost be worth it to see Mom's reaction to Brad on the couch.

Discretion prevailed. I picked up the phone.

Chapter 30

When I came downstairs the next morning, Brad was already awake and clicking through channels on the television. "How do you stand this daytime stuff?" he asked, pointing to the screen filled with jolly game show hosts and audiences evidently overdosed on laughing gas.

"Easy. I don't watch TV during the day until the weekend, and then only sports or old movies. I'll make an exception if the Cubs are ever in the play-offs again, of course." In my best Nurse Chipper voice, I asked, "And how are we feeling today? Shall I plump your pillows?"

"Hmm. I don't know about pillows, but I wouldn't mind a little plumping."

"I will ignore that insinuendo," I said.

"Insinuendo?"

"One of Mayor Daley the Elder's many malapropisms."

I reached down, and felt Brad's bare toes protruding from the splint. They were chilly. I went upstairs, got a pair of wool hiking socks, and returned. They were a bit small, but after a few snips and tugs, the sock stayed on.

"What would you like for breakfast?" I asked, running through my list of items available from the kitchen.

"I can help you," Brad said, struggling to sit up.

"Oh, no, you don't," I said. "My kitchen is too small. Too many chefs. Besides, you need to take it easy for a day or two."

§

After we ate breakfast together on trays in the living room, I made sure Brad took his medication, and settled him in with the newspaper and some magazines. As I loaded the dishwasher, the front doorbell rang. Standing on the porch were Travis Burton and Susanne Porter. "Please come in," I said.

Susanne trailed expensive perfume as I ushered the two into the living room. I called out, "Company for you, Brad!"

"Hello, again," I said. "I'm not sure we've met. I'm—"

"Yes, I know. Brad mentioned you. I do admire you working girls," she said. Working girls? Surely she must mean career women. Or was she implying I was practicing the oldest profession with Brad? I searched her face, but it gave no indication as to her meaning.

"Hi, Susanne, Travis," Brad said. "I'm so sorry to hear about Edwin."

"Thank you," said Susanne. "He was old and not in good health…."

Travis looked discomfited by her brusque dismissal of Edwin's life.

"And as if that weren't bad enough," Susanne continued, "our car was impounded by that police chief person." She rolled the word, 'person,' around her mouth like an olive pit about to be spat out.

"You know they had to go over it for evidence, Susanne. Besides, Chief Koenig was nice enough to drive us out to the car rental place for another car," said Travis. He turned to Brad and asked, "How are you? What happened?"

While Brad told them about his accident, I took a long look at Susanne and Travis. Travis, in sport jacket, black T-shirt, and tight-fitting designer jeans, leaned back in his chair, and listened as Brad talked.

Susanne appeared much as she did at the funeral home after Simon's death: perfect make-up, expensive clothes, a handbag whose price could've provided years of health care to several Third-World countries. I realized she was several years older than Travis. She perched on the edge of her chair as if expecting diseased vermin to slither out from the seat cushion at any moment. After several imperious looks around the room, which I'm sure she found *déclassé,* she looked at Travis and cleared her throat.

Susanne's signal received, Travis took a pair of glasses and some papers from his breast pocket. He put the glasses on and said, "Brad, we wanted to go over some things with you, if you're up to it."

"No problem," Brad said.

"Alone," said Susanne, with a pointed look at me.

"Of course. I'll be upstairs if you need anything."

Unlike at the funeral home, there were no draperies or other places I could skulk behind and hear what was said. I decided to clean the upstairs bathroom. It seemed like much longer than three weeks or so since I completed my tiling project, and Jake repaired the shower.

I had scrubbed the floor when Brad called, "Meg, our guests are leaving."

I went downstairs and saw them out. Susanne wrinkled her nose in disdain at my fresh, woodsy scent: Eau de Pine Sol.

§

Before I could say anything, Brad said, "That woman is certainly a piece of work."

"You took the words right out of my mouth. She certainly seems 'to the manner born.' She's a few years older than Travis, I think, but she looks good." I said.

"Like Cruella," said Brad. We both laughed.

"Do you need anything right now?" I asked. "I need to finish the bathroom."

"Nope. I haven't had a chance to read today's *Journal,* and after that, there's this stack of magazines here on the coffee table."

I went back upstairs and when I came back with the linens to wash, Brad was asleep, the newspaper on the floor where it had fallen from his hands.

§

While Brad slept, I started a list of things to get at the supermarket. I'd have to ask Brad what he liked to eat. I was restless. I couldn't leave Brad and run errands, and I didn't have any more information about the Porter murders to send Harry. The day was gray and overcast, the trees almost bare of their autumn splendor. Rain was forecast. Much as I hated to leave my cozy kitchen, I thought I'd better get my canoe and kayak put away. I doubted I would use the canoe again until spring, but the kayak was smaller and lighter, so I'd put the kayak right inside the door of the shed. There'd be some nice days before the lake froze in the coming winter.

Dressed in my barn jacket over my clothes, gloves, and boots, I walked over to the shore, where both boats were pulled up on the sand beach.

First, the canoe. It was about sixteen feet long, sat two, and was perfect for recreational paddling on our small lake. The down side was that it weighed about eighty pounds. A few years ago, Dad rigged a pulley system for me to haul it into the shed. I turned the boat right-side up, took out the paddles, attached the lines, and pulled.

About fifteen minutes later, the canoe was secured in the shed.

The one-person kayak was light, so I could carry it. I laid the paddle to one side. As I turned over the boat and hoisted it, upside-down, over my head, debris rained down on me from inside the boat. Yuck. I returned to the shed, grabbed some rags from behind a stack of window screens, and wiped out the kayak. When the boats and paddles were put away, I stood on the dock for a bit and watched sluggish ripples on the leaden water. I shivered and went inside.

§

Brad was sipping coffee at the kitchen table, his crutches propped against the wall, when I got inside.

"Should you be up and around so soon?" I asked.

"Been practicing with my crutches. Only fell three times." He looked at my stricken face. "Just kidding, Meg."

"I was thinking of doing a little shopping," I said, "as soon as I change my clothes and clean up a bit."

"What were you doing outside? That wind was chilly when you came in the door," said Brad.

"I put away the kayak and the canoe in the shed."

I washed my hands at the sink and said, "Brad, I'm thinking we may have overlooked the obvious in the two murders."

"In what way?" he asked.

"The TV detective shows—"

"Uh-oh," Brad said, laughing. "I shudder to think what's coming."

I laughed too, and then continued, "They always say that the spouse is often the culprit."

"Edwin's wife has been dead more than twenty years," Brad said.

"You know what I mean. Travis and Susanne are having an affair. Maybe she talked him into killing Simon."

"Wouldn't a divorce be easier?" asked Brad.

"Well, yes, unless there was a pre-nuptial agreement between Simon and Susanne."

"Actually, there was one," said Brad.

"Aha!"

"Their pre-nup was to protect Susanne's money. She's a rich woman, Meg. Old money, Lake Forest, the whole bit."

"Well, you know Simon and Marlene were also having a fling," I countered, "although I don't see Simon tossing away his marriage for Marlene."

"Simon never could keep his pants zipped," Brad said.

He and I sat in silence for a while.

"Who benefits from Simon and Edwin both being dead?" I asked.

"There being no children from Simon's marriage, it's tricky. If Edwin had died first, then his money would pass to Simon, and from there to Susanne," Brad said, "Assuming a traditional will."

"Except Susanne, from what you've said, has wealth of her own."

"But Simon was killed first, so whatever he had will pass to Susanne, who doesn't need the money."

"With Simon gone first, I wonder who inherits whatever Edwin left," I said. "Susanne?"

"That I doubt very much," said Brad. "There was no love lost between Edwin and Susanne. Simon's father never forgave him for marrying a *shiksa,* and she's made some nasty remarks about Jews. If there aren't any relatives, maybe Edwin left the money to one of the Jewish charities he supported.

"One thing I know for sure. I wish I could've avoided getting involved with the disposition of Simon's remains. It was complicated for a non-Jew like me. Still, I was glad to help."

"What about Edwin's body?" I asked. "It's still with the coroner, right?"

"Right," said Brad. "The coroner told me he's going to ask Winn Jacobson to contact Edwin's temple in Chicago this time. Have them handle the details."

"Sad thing," I said, "having no family members to mourn you." I gave myself a mental shake and said, "So who gets Porter-Burton Enterprises? Travis is the only named partner left. Is the company his now? If so, he's free to marry Susanne and her money, and continue with the Prairie Lake development."

"Only one problem," said Brad. "Travis was with me the night Simon was killed."

"Well, drat!" I said.

Brad smiled. "After the town hall meeting, Simon told us he'd forgotten some blueprints he wanted to look over. Someone, Simon didn't say who, offered to take him there after the meeting, wait while he picked up the prints, and drive him back to the hotel in town. So, I saw you safely out of the town-hall parking lot, I drove Travis and Edwin back to the Palace. The three of us re-hashed the town-hall meeting fiasco over a couple of drinks. We didn't think much about Simon's not returning, thought he'd maybe bought a night-cap for the person who was nice enough to take him to the yard."

"When we were at the construction yard the day the body was discovered, you suggested to Chief Koenig that he look into how Simon got to the yard the night before. When I'm in town, I'll drop by the police station and ask Billy if they found out who gave Simon a lift after the meeting at the town hall," I said.

"It's worth a try, but he probably didn't find out anything," said Brad.

Brad and I stared at each other. We shared the same thought. The person who drove Simon to the construction yard that night was his killer, and the killer wouldn't offer the ride in front of any witnesses.

I changed my clothes, grabbed my car keys, and started out the door. Brad handed me his credit card. "My treat," he said. "Oh, and would you mind stopping at my house and picking up my shaving stuff and some clothes?" he asked, rubbing the stubble on his chin.

"Surely, Mr. Trinder," I teased, "you haven't left your house unlocked?"

He handed me his keys. "Don't get smart with me, woman, or I'll swat you with a crutch."

"You'll have to catch me first."

§

The Bramble police station was my first stop. It was Saturday, so Ella, the full-time receptionist, wasn't on duty. A patrolman staffed the desk. He looked up. "Yes?"

"Is Chief Koenig in?" I asked.

"On a Saturday?" The young officer smirked. "What do you need, ma'am?"

"I'm Meg Smyth, with the *Journal-Times.* I'm following up on the Porter murders."

The patrolman's eyes grew wary. "I'm not at liberty to—"

A police officer with dark hair and eyes, and wearing a white uniform shirt bearing the stripes of a sergeant, came over to us from where he'd been sitting at the other end of the counter, and said, "Hi, Meg! What's up?" The patrol officer threw him a grateful look and backed away.

"Hi, George. Just looking for an update on the murders," I said. George Cadotte was part Chippewa, his Native American ancestors intermarrying with French traders who came to this part of the country.

"I'll tell you what I can," said George. "It's an ongoing investigation, so I can't tell you too much."

"Did the person who drove Simon Porter to the construction yard come forward? Or was he identified?"

"Nope. We asked around, but nothing new has turned up," he replied.

"What about Edwin Porter?"

"Some trace inside the car," George said, "but don't put that in the paper. It was a rental car, so the stuff could've been there for months, belonged to anyone who'd rented it." He paused, "Off the record…"

"Of course."

"Coupla odd things," he said.

I gave him a quizzical look. "What do you mean?"

"Well, both Simon and Edwin Porter were found at the construction yard after they'd gone there late at night. We know Simon went to the yard to get some blueprints. Simon didn't have the rental car the night he was killed, and it looks like we'll never find out who drove him there. The crime scene was so scuffed up from various vehicles…

"Anyway," George continued, "Edwin Porter's body was found near his rental car, but why would he be at the yard so late? It's hard to believe he would give a lift to someone he didn't know—especially after his son was killed by someone who gave him a ride."

"Maybe he met someone there," I suggested. There were a lot of unanswered questions.

I thought of the logic problem about the fox, the chicken, and the bag of grain: how to move the three items from one point to another, two at a time, without the chicken eating the grain, or the fox eating the chicken. The logistics of the murders were hard to figure out, yet seemed integral to the solving them.

"That's the best answer we've come up with, too," George said. "But what could possibly have been so important that he would meet someone there at night, especially—"

"After what happened to his son, Simon," I finished. "The two deaths are linked, I suppose?"

"Almost certain. Edwin Porter still had his wallet, credit cards, and an expensive watch. No car keys. Had to call the Lincoln-Mercury dealership in Walnut Creek to tow it to the county building."

"Was Edwin killed at the site?" I asked.

"Hard to tell. His head was bashed in—" George stopped and eyed me.

"It's okay, George, I can handle it. I've got a strong stomach."

"The coroner says there would have been some blood, but nowhere near as much as there was with a bullet wound like Simon's."

I thought for a minute. "Are you sure that the same person killed both Simon and Edwin Porter?"

"I sure hope so," George said.

I stared at him. "What?"

"I'd hate to think there are two murderers loose in Bramble."

Chapter 31

Henry's Supermarket was almost empty this late on a Saturday afternoon, so I managed to get my shopping done quickly. I headed for an open register. There was no one ahead of me in the checkout line. I unloaded my groceries before I noticed there was no cashier in the checkout line. Henry himself hastened over, knelt down on the floor behind the belt, and, crawling around, began gathering into his hands miles of cash-register tape curled on the floor. His head popped up. He looked like a mummy unraveling. "Sorry about this. It'll be ready in a minute." A minute in dog's years.

§

It was dark when I reached Brad's house. I had hoped to be here before nightfall to get the things he wanted. My last visit here put me in the hospital. I grabbed the empty suitcase I had brought from home, and walked up to the front door. There was a lamp on in the living room, but I was still trepidant as I unlocked the door and went inside.

Brad had been busy while I was in the hospital. The floors were swept and the cobwebs gone. A table and three chairs replaced the broken furniture. The fireplace had been cleaned, a fire built, and ready to light. In the kitchen, the sink and counters were scrubbed and free of caked-on ook. No trace of mice. The rusty refrigerator had been removed and a new one stood in its place. I went over to the stairs and saw that two or three treads had been replaced with new wood. The billowing wallpaper had been removed. Still cautious with my footing, and holding tightly to the railing, I headed upstairs.

A smaller bedroom in the front of the house was empty. Brad had moved his things into the larger bedroom overlooking the lake. I found a wall switch, which turned on a ceiling light. Against one wall was a cot, neatly made up with a couple of blankets and a pillow. A small table was next to it.

Two chipped and scratched dressers stood against the wall. They probably were in the house when Brad rented it. I walked over to the larger of the two, and opened the top drawer. Brad's socks were matched and rolled, military-style. The next drawer held loosely folded underwear. I noted he preferred boxers and V-necked undershirts. I felt intrusive as I scooped up a week's supply of underthings. I opened and closed the drawers of both dressers methodically. Finding no pajamas, I wondered if he slept commando. Hmm…

Enough, Meg. On to the closet. Most of the things on the hangers and shelves were fairly new. I surmised that Brad bought them after he learned he would be in the area awhile. His taste ran toward Eddie Bauer, although there were two nice sports jackets, some slacks, a suit, and some dress shirts. I grabbed the jeans, sweaters, and a couple of flannel shirts from the shelf. I managed to catch a framed photograph before it fell to the floor. I held it up. Smiling from the photo was a younger Brad, his arm around a woman holding a baby. Was this his ex-wife? His child? He hadn't mentioned anything about children, but then, we hadn't had a lot of time to talk about our personal lives. I put the picture back on the shelf.

The suitcase was full. I turned and looked back at the room to make sure I had left things in order. I turned off the light, went downstairs, and locked up.

§

Brad opened the kitchen door for me. "Hi, I saw you coming. I'm not sure I'll be much help," he said, tottering a bit on his crutches.

"No problem. If you'll hold the door, I'll get your stuff and the groceries inside."

Several trips later, Brad's clothes were stuffed into the hall closet, and the food put away. I fed Minerva, and asked Brad, "What would you like to eat?"

"You've been running around all day, Meg," he said. "How 'bout we order a pizza tonight and stay warm and cozy?"

I didn't need much coaxing, as I was a bit chilled. "Deal!" I said. "I'll take a shower while you order the pizza." I lifted a magnet on the refrigerator, and handed the take-out menu to him.

"What would you like on the pizza?" Brad asked.

"No anchovies or pineapple. Anything else you want to get is fine. Be sure to tell him to come to the back door, in case the delivery guy gets here before I'm out of the shower. I picked up some soft drinks at the store. They're in the refrigerator. There's beer in there too, but that's off-limits while you're still taking painkillers." Gee, I sound bossy.

Brad grinned. "Yes, ma'am."

I fished out my credit card from my purse, and plunked on the table. Before Brad could protest, I said, "My treat this time."

Were it not for the prospect of food—somehow, I had missed lunch—I would've stayed under the hot water until sometime the next week. I put on sweats and my fuzzy slippers, dried my hair, came downstairs, and joined Brad at the kitchen table. The pizza arrived and we fell on it as if we hadn't eaten since dinosaurs roamed the earth.

Brad and I talked for a while until his painkillers caught up with him. I helped him up from his chair. He put his crutches under his arms and clumped into the downstairs powder room, and from there to his makeshift bed on the couch. I turned and retired upstairs.

I'm one of those people who are usually cold, even on the hottest days. My old house was chilly to me, so I put a turtle-necked shirt on under my flannel granny gown. So sexy.

Sexy. That brought my thoughts around to Brad. I wanted to ask him about the photograph, but wanted to think it over first. I vacillated about my feelings toward him. Was it lust? Love? How did I feel about the possibility of Brad having a child or children? The photo was several years old. The child in the photo would be somewhere between eight and ten now. How can I approach him with my questions? I tossed about on a sea of rumpled sheets, until I finally dropped off to sleep.

§

The lake was shrouded in fog the next morning. I could barely see the dock. Ominous clouds bunched in the west. Brad and I had finished breakfast when Jon and Louis, dropped by, their arms laden with trays, bags, and packages. I cleared some counter space, and the two began unpacking.

Jon said to Brad, "Meg only has a kitchen because the house came with one, so we thought you might need something more tantalizing to sustain you." Jon eyed with disdain the empty pizza box in the garbage can. "I see we were right."

"I went to Henry's yesterday," I said in my defense.

"Henry's? The supermarket?" asked Louis. His tone placed Henry's on the same epicurean level as an abattoir.

I made no reply.

Louis looked inside my refrigerator. "I see cheese, milk, what appears to be a slab of mystery meat, and some unsuccessful science experiments." He opened the freezer compartment. "Ooh, lots of little 'gourmet' low-cal treats for your microwave." He shook his head. The pair loaded my refrigerator and pantry with wonderful things from the Heron, complete with cooking instructions.

Jon said, "We also came over to see if we could run any errands, be of help somehow."

"Oh, guys," I said. "This is more than enough."

"Meg's right," Brad agreed. He paused. "Although…I have a follow-up appointment with the orthopedist tomorrow. I think they'll give me a boot to replace this splint thing. Meg's been running herself ragged. If one of you is available…"

"Say no more," said Louis. "We're closed on Mondays, so we are yours to command." The three men made plans to take Brad to his appointment.

A gust of wind rattled the kitchen window. "Looks like we're in for some 'filthy weather,' as the Brits say," said Louis.

"Good night to snuggle and watch an old flick," said Jon. He turned to Louis, "We still have *It Happened One Night* we borrowed from the Bramble Library."

"Mmm, Clark Gable and Claudette Colbert," Louis said. "Reminds me of Max and Claudie Trent."

Jon and Brad looked stupefied. "How can Gable and Colbert possibly remind you of the Trents?" asked Brad.

"I know! I know!" I said, waving my hand in the air like the obnoxious teacher's pet I was in the third grade.

"Claudie Trent's first name is…" I paused.

"Claudette!" Louis and I said together.

Jon and Brad exchanged a look casting doubt on our sanity. I told the men about Claudie's mother being a fan of Claudette Colbert.

Jon said to me, "You know that Claudie left Max a week or so ago? Ran off with a woman to Florida?"

"A woman?" I was flabbergasted. I thought back to the conversation I'd overheard between Marlene Tigran and Claudie at Sally's party. "I kinda thought Claudie was after Simon Porter."

"No, Meg, dear," said Jon. "Before I met Louis, I noticed Claudie from time to time at one of the, um, bars in Walnut Creek."

"The Heron and the Liberty Café use the same soft-drink distributor," said Louis. "From what he's told me, Max is worried about the Prairie Lake development, now that Edwin's dead too."

"Max thought his ship had come in," I said. "He has big plans for expanding the motel."

"He's hired someone full-time to run Sleepytime," said Louis. "That must be a strain on the budget. Claudie worked for nothing." Nothing except money and jewelry from blackmailing Marlene Tigran.

After many thank-yous from Brad and me, Louis and Jon left to open up their restaurant.

They were gone only a few minutes when Pete Winters, accompanied by his two twin sons, knocked at the door. I was glad they missed each other, given Pete's antipathy toward gays.

"Hi, Pete, guys. Come on in," I said.

"Thanks, but no," Pete said. He nodded to Brad, "I'm actually here to see your, uh, friend. I heard about your accident and that you were here. Wondered if you finished the roof repair before your mishap. If not, me and my boys here could take a look at it, patch it up. I do odd jobs like that in addition to my septic system service."

"Hey, thanks, Pete," Brad said. "I think it's okay, but the true test will be next time we have a downpour."

"Well, let me know if you need help," Pete said. He walked off down the lane toward his home, his two sons lumbering after him.

"That was nice," Brad said.

"Living in a small town has its advantages, that's for sure," I said.

Pete Winters was a bigot, but was he also a killer? Did he kill Simon Porter? Pete had motive—his rabid and violent aversion to the Prairie Lake development plans. He had means—was his nine-millimeter Glock really taken from his truck? He had opportunity—he was home alone after the high-school football game was cancelled. What about Edwin Porter's homicide? Same means and motive for killing Simon. Where was Pete when Edwin was killed?

§

Brad and I dug out some sandwiches and a salad from the goodies Louis and Jon left, and sat down to lunch. The phone rang. Somehow, I knew it was Mom.

"Hi, Mom," I said. "How are you? And Dad?"

Mom wasted no time on social chitchat. "That second murder you phoned us about is in our papers out here. What's going on? We should be with you."

"No need to come back here, Mom. It's under control. The police have lots of leads," I said.

Brad looked up. "They do?"

I gestured for him to shush. Too late. Mom asked, "Who is that with you? That nice young man?"

"No, Mom, it's just the radio."

Brad grinned.

"How is Brad, by the way? Have you seen him again?"

"Oh, I see him from time to time." On my couch.

Brad grinned again. He got up and started toward me.

"Well, gotta go, Mom. I have something in the oven."

"Something in the oven?" I visualized Mom's look of amazement. The idea of me cooking was probably more shocking to her than if she learned of my foray into Brad's underwear drawer.

"Yes, Jon and Louis dropped off some food left over from the Heron. I'm warming it up," I said. Brad had wrapped his arms around me. "Don't worry, Mom. Everything's fine here."

I hung up the phone and turned. Brad drew me closer, his warm breath against my neck. His lips were soft as he kissed me. I could feel his growing urgency as he pressed his body against mine.

"Dammit!" I said.

"What?" he murmured in my ear.

"There's someone at the front door. I heard the bell ring."

"Ignore them," Brad said, his voice husky.

"I can't. Whoever it is will come to the back door and see us…"

We pulled away from each other, and I answered the door.

§

"Pastor Joe!" I said. "Come in, come in."

As Pastor Jenkins settled himself in an armchair in the living room, Brad whispered to me, "Perhaps we should book a quiet getaway weekend in Grand Central Station."

"How are you, Brad?" asked Pastor Joe. "Heard you were staying here while your leg mended." I sighed. Even the pastor knew that I had a male live-in guest.

"May I get you something to drink?" I asked. "I have coffee or…"

"No, no, thank you. I can't stay." I saw Brad grin behind Pastor Joe's back. His cheerful look vanished as Pastor Joe continued, "Marlene Tigran tried to take her own life, Meg."

"Oh, no!" I sat down. "What happened?"

"Late yesterday afternoon, Jake drove the kids over to Marlene's mother's house in Sutton Valley for an sleep-over. Her community has an indoor swimming pool, which the kids love, especially at this time of year. She takes the kids from time to time, partly to give Marlene and Jake some time alone, mostly because she adores her grandchildren.

"When Jake returned, he found Marlene unconscious in their bedroom. There were empty pill bottles in the bathroom. Jake couldn't rouse her, so he took her to the hospital himself. He was afraid that calling the paramedics would take too long. Anyway, the ER people pumped her stomach, and eventually, she regained consciousness."

"Did she say why? Or leave a note?" I asked.

"I don't know. Jake didn't say. He's been frantic, blames himself."

"Is she at home?"

"No, the hospital wanted to keep her another night or two, perhaps do a psych evaluation," Pastor Joe said. He cleared his throat. "Meg, the reason I'm here is I wondered if you'd go visit her. She doesn't have many women friends, and I saw you talking with her at Sally's party."

"Of course, if you don't think Jake would mind."

"He's at a loss over this. I think he'd be grateful for anyone who might be able to help Marlene. She hasn't said much. Maybe she'd talk with you."

§

After Pastor Jenkins left, I turned to Brad. "I—"

Brad came over and gave me a gentle kiss. "Shh. Go and see Marlene. She needs you."

"You're sure you'll be all right?"

"Absolutely. I'll plunk down here and watch the Bears game."

I changed my clothes and got in the car. As I drove over to the hospital, Brad's words came back to me, "She needs you, too." What did the "too" mean?

I found a place to park near the main entrance of the hospital, and hurried in. I was spending far too much time here recently.

Marlene was sitting up in bed when I arrived. She looked as if she'd aged fifteen years. Her red hair was dull and hung in snarls around her face. Her face was colorless, her eyes vacant. I went over and put my hand over hers.

"Hi, Marlene," I said. I stopped, not sure how to proceed with someone who had made up her mind to leave this world.

"Hello, Meg," said the wraith in the bed. "Good of you to come. I really messed up this time." Her voice was hoarse, probably from the procedures she underwent in the Emergency Room.

"Nothing happened that can't be put right, Marlene. You have another chance." I felt I was mouthing clichés.

"Claudie…" said Marlene. "She…"

"What happened?" I asked.

"She left town with some woman she was having an affair with at the motel." Marlene gave a short, barking laugh. "And she was blackmailing *me* over Simon Porter. Weird, huh?"

I nodded and squeezed her hand.

"Yeah, well, before she left, she told Jake about Simon and me. I didn't have no more money to give her…"

"Oh, Marlene, I'm so sorry."

"Well, Jake didn't believe her at first. He asked me. I tried to lie, but he knew I wasn't telling the truth. He took the kids to my mother's house so we could talk without them hearing us. I couldn't face him, so before he got back..." Marlene began to cry.

I handed her a tissue, and sat quietly for a while, patting her hand.

Jake came in, carrying the most enormous bouquet of flowers I'd ever seen. He walked over and kissed Marlene on the cheek. I got up to leave.

"Meg, thank you for coming. It means a lot to me and Marlene," he said. He walked me out to the hall.

"Jake, I'm so sorry," I said.

"I don't know what I'd do without Marlene," he said. "I love her so much." Tears started in his eyes. "I know I've not been home as much as I could to help out. That Simon Porter is—was—a slime ball, but I see how Marlene could be attracted to him. Smooth, city-like. I don't care what she did. I love her."

"Just tell her that, Jake. Over and over. Every day," I said. I never thought my Miss Polly advice mantra would ever be needed by anyone I knew.

I drove home, thinking of Jake and Marlene. Good people going through a rough patch. I had a feeling they'd work things out.

§

The football game was nearly over when I arrived home. I glanced at the quarter-by-quarter score displayed on the television screen. The Bears had snatched defeat from the jaws of victory once again.

"Hi, Meg. Watching the Bears is a painful experience," Brad said, turning off the television. "How did things go at the hospital?" Brad moved over so I could sit on the couch next to him. He put his arm around my shoulders, and I leaned into him. I told him about my conversations with Marlene and Jake.

"Let's have a bite to eat," Brad said. "And then we need to talk. There are some things you should know about me." I thought of the photograph I'd come across at his house. It was time to talk.

§

After dinner, I brought a tray with coffee and some lighter-than-air lemon meringue tarts Jon and Louis brought that morning. So full was the day, that I was amazed their visit was only this morning. I stirred some cream into my coffee, took a sip, and waited for Brad to start.

"Meg, it's been several years since I've cared about a woman in the way I care about you," he said, searching my face.

I smiled into his eyes, and he continued, "Okay, brief history of Brad Trinder. Very brief. I have other plans for the evening, my pretty." He twirled a non-existent mustache. "I grew up in Kensington, Maryland, just outside D.C. Dad worked in the Attorney General's office, and Mom stayed home with us kids. My folks still live in the house I grew up in. I have two brothers, Luke and Chuck. I'm the middle kid. Luke's a couple of years younger than I am, Chuck's about three years older.

"I commuted to the University of Maryland, majored in business. I had good grades and no arrest record, so I was recruited by the FBI." Seeing my look, he said, "Most FBI jobs are pretty dull: accounting, intelligence analysis, information technology, and so forth.

"As you know, I got married. Nikki—Nicole—and I met in college at her senior recital. She's a wonderful contralto. She opted to teach, rather than pursue a performance career. She taught at the high school in Silver Spring until our daughter was born. We named her Jennifer Lynn. Sort of a musical play on words, like Jenny Lind, the Swedish singer."

I nodded. "Clever, especially since Nikki was a singer too. How old is Jennifer now?"

Brad's eyes darkened. "She would have been eight years old in a couple of weeks. She died of Sudden Infant Death Syndrome."

"Oh, Brad." I squeezed his arm. "I'm so sorry."

"My job took me all over the country, and I wasn't home when it happened," Brad said. "Nikki blamed me, the job, for Jenny's death. If I'd been there, if Nikki hadn't been so exhausted trying to cope with an infant by herself..."

"Brad—"

"No, she was right. At least, about my job. And to be honest, I said some pretty nasty things to Nikki, too. Her parents wouldn't speak to me, even at the funeral. Anyway, Nikki and I went to a counselor, tried to patch things up, went to a SIDS support group. In the end, our marriage couldn't withstand the pain, the guilt."

We sat in silence for a long while.

I said, "Well, you've met my parents. I also have a younger brother, Jim. He's been what I guess you'd call 'estranged' from our family. He got into drugs in college, dropped out. He's been in and out of rehab a couple of times, but he hasn't contacted any of us in over a year."

"Oh, Meg, that has to be hard on you and your parents. Do you have any idea where he is?"

"He was in Chicago living with some group, almost like a commune, I guess. He's always been secretive about his friends."

"I could make some inquiries," Brad said.

"Maybe. I'd have to check with my parents, first. Jim stole quite a bit of money from them, forging checks. They never prosecuted, but they may not want to open that particular can of worms."

"I understand," Brad said. "Let me know if you want me to look into his whereabouts."

I cleared my throat, and tried for a lighter note. "As for me, I'm a spinster."

"Hardly!"

"Well, legally, I am. That's how my house title reads." I went on to tell him about Matt. "I'm one of many women who put their guys through school, only to be dumped. I've had a few dalliances since then, but nothing really serious."

"Only a writer would use 'dalliances' to describe her torrid affairs," Brad chuckled. He cupped my chin and looked at me, "This Matt guy was a fool to let you go, Meg."

I pulled his face to mine and kissed him. His tongue explored my mouth as his hands reached under my sweater. As I reached down to unzip his pants, Brad shifted his position to help me. And rolled off the couch.

"Are you okay? Are you hurt?" I asked.

He managed to sit up on the floor. "I'm fine," he said. "The best laid plans—"

"So to speak," I said.

We laughed and agreed the moment was lost.

Chapter 32

After our romantic fiasco the night before, I wasn't sure how things would be between Brad and me the next morning. I thought back to a couple of times with Matt when our sexual encounters didn't go as hoped. He never could laugh about it, and usually blamed me.

"Good morning, Meg," he said as he hobbled into the kitchen, and gave me a lingering kiss. "I think I provided a new definition of 'couch potato' last night. I'm really sorry, Meg. I guess I forgot about the splint in the heat of the moment."

I hugged him. It felt so good to be in a man's arms. I said, "We can always turn up the heat again."

"I'll get this splint off, and be a new man."

"Or a nude man," I said.

"Even better," Brad replied.

§

Jon Dreher came by around noon to drive Brad to the doctor. I resolved to use my time alone to tidy up the living room a bit. If all went well with his leg, Brad wouldn't be sleeping on the couch any more. I brushed aside several indecent ideas that sprang to mind, and started picking up newspapers, dishes, and other detritus from his convalescence. I straightened the stack of magazines and I saw Brad hadn't taken his gun with him. When I opened the drawer of the end table, I noticed a manila envelope—the information Harry Josten had given me about Porter-Burton Enterprises. I tucked it away when my parents visited and never gave it another thought. I opened it and moved to a chair to look through the material.

I sifted through several feature stories about Edwin Porter and his partnership with Henry Burton, Travis's father. They had met in Europe, where they worked as laborers clearing rubble after the war. Eventually, the two men emigrated from Europe to the United States, where they started PBE in pursuit of the American dream. Edwin changed his Polish surname from Pasziewicz to Porter, so Americans could spell and pronounce it. The company started small, both Porter and Burton working long hours to save enough money to buy property and equipment. More recent pictures showed Simon and Susanne at their wedding at the Ambassador East in Chicago and at various black-tie charity galas since then. Travis Burton was profiled a couple of times in the business section of the *Journal-Times,* but didn't seem to be part of the socialite scene.

Jon told us Marlene Tigran had been released earlier in the day, and was at home. I'd liked to see Marlene again, but today would be too early. She and her family needed some time together.

Brad and Jon wouldn't be back for a few hours, so I thought I'd drive over to the hospital and look in on Gita Banicki. I had meant to stop in to see her the other day when I visited Marlene, but the time had slipped away. It was beginning to rain again as I grabbed my coat from the hook and opened the door. I glanced back and saw Minerva glaring at me from her food dish. As she often did, she ate all the food in the middle of the dish, leaving the rest of the food circled around the bowl's vacant center. To her mind, this constituted an empty food dish and imminent starvation. I added more food, scratched her head a couple of times, and left.

§

The rain picked up and my windshield wipers had difficulty keeping up with the downpour. Something niggled at me on my way to the hospital. I was distracted and needed to think. I didn't want to end up in a ditch, so I pulled into the drug store lot. I dashed inside. Sitting in a booth, I ordered coffee and reviewed what I knew about Edwin Porter. Edwin Porter was Polish. So was Gita Banicki. Both were Jewish. Was there a connection? I closed my eyes and visualized him at the town meeting, and again at Memory Meadows. Dear God, I've gone about this all wrong. It's all about misdirection.

I pulled out my Nokia, raised its antenna, and made a phone call.

§

Sally greeted me from the desk where she was sorting books. "Hi, Meg! How's Brad?"

"Getting better. He should be much more mobile after he sees the orthopod today."

"Mobile, huh?" She gave me a knowing look.

"Don't even think about going there."

She laughed. "What brings you out on such a miserable day?"

"A little research. I need to look up something." I pulled up a chair to the computer and looked up the books I needed, and lugged them from the reference section to a table. After a short while, I found what I wanted and made a note of it. As the librarians preferred, I left the books on the table for reshelving.

I waved to Sally on my way out.

§

I took the elevator to the ICU floor, where Gita Banicki still was in a coma. I sat for a while at her bedside. Tubes ran in and out of her arms, her concentration camp tattoo obscured by the tape holding them in place. I gently lifted the tape, and said aloud, "It's the same as—"

"Hello, Meg," A voice behind me said. "Same as what?"

I started. "Oh, hello, Tony. I came by to see how your mother's doing."

"She's declining," he replied. "I don't know how much longer…"

"I'm so sorry, Tony," I said. "Please let me know if there's anything I can do."

§

One more stop. Darkness set in earlier at this time of year, and shop lights were coming on up and down Main Street. I found a slot in front of the Bushel O'Bargains. No customers were inside.

Mad dogs and Englishmen were noonday-sun crazy. I was cold-and-rainy crazy. I picked out a couple of bottles of wine for the evening. Brad was off the painkillers, and I was hoping we'd continue where we'd left off the night before. I handed the store clerk my credit card. Ounce for ounce, the cost of wine from the gourmet shop came close to exceeding the price of gold.

§

I drove as fast as I dared, my car hydroplaning and skidding as I sped around corners. The sky took on a sickly greenish-yellow cast. Thunder rumbled overhead and the sky was inky with black clouds. Lightning crackled, illuminating the sky with flickering instants of purple.

I ran toward the house, opened the door, and stood dripping and shivering inside as I hung up my jacket and slipped off my sodden shoes and socks. Rain pelted the windows. The ash tree on the side of my house tapped its fingers on the roof. My old refrigerator groaned into silence. The power went off.

Power outages were nothing new in Bramble. I kept matches and a kerosene lamp in a kitchen cabinet. As I reached for the cabinet handle, a powerful hand wrenched me backward in the darkness.

Chapter 33

I struggled. My wet, bare feet slid on the floor. I smelled my assailant's sour breath. A fork of lightning flashed and cast a flickering light on his face. Tony Banicki.

"Tony, please—" I said.

"Sit down, Meg," he said, pushing me onto a kitchen chair. "You really should lock your doors." I must've forgotten to lock it after I fed Minerva.

"You'd better get out of here. Brad will be back any moment," I said.

"I don't think so," Tony said. "On the way here from the hospital, I saw him and Jon Dreher trying to fix a flat tire on their car. By the time they get here, it will be too late." My stomach lurched. Dear God, Tony intended to kill me.

"I have a kerosene lamp in the cabinet," I said, "and some matches. I was just getting them. Would you like—?"

"Yes, that would be fine, Meg. I'd like to see what I'm doing." Tony spoke softly, which terrified me more than if he shouted. "Bring them here. Slowly. I have a gun, so don't try to do anything foolish," he said.

I walked over to the cabinet, took out the lamp and matches, and carried them to the table. My hands shook so badly, I had to strike the match three or four times before I could light the wick. I replaced the lamp's chimney, and turned up the flame.

"Not so high, Meg. A nice, soft glow will be better, don't you think?" I turned down the wick and forced myself to meet Tony's eyes. A glint played in them: a trick of the light or was Tony gripped by madness?

In his hand, Tony held a gun pointed at me. My mind raced. How could I wrest it away from him? My eyes strayed to the lamp on the kitchen table.

"Don't try anything, Meg," he said, as if reading my mind. "There really is no escape. Not any more."

I had to stall, keep him talking. Please, Brad and Jon, get here. I willed them to flag down a motorist, walk somewhere for help. But Brad couldn't walk far without help, and no one was out in this storm. I brightened for a moment. Surely, one of them had a mobile phone. Problem was that phone signals here were weak, often displaying "no signal," even on nice days. In any event, the two men didn't know Ms. Independent needed help, so they wouldn't be in a hurry to get back here. Maybe they'd wait out the storm. Or someone would pick them up and they'd all go somewhere for a few drinks or dinner. A tear rolled down my cheek. You cannot give up, Meg. I took a deep breath and asked, "What do you mean, Tony?"

He pointed to a deep gouge on the tabletop. "See this, Meg?"

"Yes."

"You could fill this with wood filler, stain it, and no one would see it any more."

"Yes?"

"But underneath, the flaw would still be there." His eyes burned into mine, the flame from the lamp reflected in them. "That's how it is with evil. You can cover it up, but it's still there."

"I'm not sure I understand, Tony," I said.

Tony sighed. "It's a long story, Meg, but you might as well hear it before…" A chill ran up my spine. I shivered. Tony got up and walked over to the door, grabbed a sweatshirt off the hook, and handed it to me. "You're cold. I hate to see you suffer, Meg. And I promise, you won't." He smiled as I pulled the shirt on. "There. See? Cozy. I keep Mother cozy too, you know."

"You're a good son, Tony," I said.

"Thank you, Meg," he said. "I tried to keep the evil from her, but I couldn't…"

"Tell me about the evil, about your mother," I said, fascinated, yet repelled, by this man seated across the table from me.

"It was at the bank that Mother saw him. Edwin Porter."

Tony gave me a sly look. "That's what he called himself now, but Mother knew him by another name: Edwin Pasziewicz." Porter's original Polish name I'd seen in the *Journal* material Harry Josten had given me.

"Your mother knew Edwin from Auschwitz, from Birkenau, didn't she?"

I'd remembered that although the weather was warm, Edwin wore long sleeves at the town meeting and at Memory Meadows. I'd called the police station earlier today and George confirmed Edwin had a faint tattoo on his forearm, and gave me the numbers. My research at the library gave me information on the numbers used at the various camps. When I visited Gita at the hospital, I saw that her tattoo and Edwin's indicated they were in the same camp. Tony must've heard my comment about his mother's arm, and realized I was a threat to him.

"Yes. Auschwitz-Birkenau, a combination extermination and forced-labor camp. Not that it made much difference: being gassed or dying from abuse or starvation." Tony's eyes glittered with hatred.

"He was a *kapo*," Tony said. "*Kapos* were Jewish prisoners who were given special privileges for helping the SS keep the prisoners under control. This reduced the number of Nazi guards necessary in the camp."

Kapo. That's what Gita was saying when Sally and I visited her. Tony was clever. He covered his mother's words by leading us believe Gita was confused and talking about *cops* on television.

"But weren't these *kapos* forced to do this? They were Jewish. Weren't they threatened too?" I asked.

"Some *kapos* were good and obtained extra rations and clothing for the others. Some were brutal."

"And Edwin?"

"I don't know which he was. He got away in the confusion when the Soviets liberated Birkenau in 1945," Tony replied.

"So Edwin might've been doing what he could to help the others?"

"It doesn't matter!" He waved the gun. "Don't you understand? I had to protect *Matka*, Mother. We came here to this little village in the middle of the United States to be safe, to be as far away as possible from the horrors of Birkenau. And there in town was this man from her past, walking around. Mother was confused, terrified.

"Mother goes to bed early, and that night, I gave her a sedative. After she was asleep, I went to the meeting at the town hall. Even though there were people who protested the construction project, it was evident to me that there was no chance PBE would stop the development and leave. They mentioned talking with us one-on-one."

"So you offered Simon Porter a ride?"

"Very smart of you, Meg," he smiled and patted my hand. It took every ounce of will power I had not to scream at his touch. "Yes, I overheard him say he needed to go to the construction yard to pick up some blueprints. Simon was, as you Americans say, the 'mover and shaker' behind the project, so I thought perhaps I could persuade him to abandon the project."

"How could you do that?" I asked.

"After we were inside the construction trailer, I threatened to tell everyone that his father had been a *kapo.*

"Simon argued with me, said that I only had my mother's word that his father was anything but a prisoner just like Mother. 'Just like Mother,' he said. Edwin Porter was rich, giving money to Jewish causes, a big shot. While Mother was…"

Spittle formed at the corner of Tony Banicki's mouth, "I went toward Simon and he pulled a gun from behind a counter. This gun," Tony said, waving the weapon in his hand. "I didn't go there to kill Simon, but he was evil. I got the gun away from him and shot him."

Tony told his grisly story with no inflection. He might have been reading listings in a telephone book. I was alone with a madman. Thunder and lightning crashed outside. I heard a branch from a tree outside break off with a crack and fall to the ground. The roads were probably flooded and impassable. Brad, where are you?

"So," I said, my voice coming out as a croak, "you carried Simon out to the yard and arranged him in the backhoe so his murder would look like it was related to the development?"

"Oh, no, Meg." Tony gave a little laugh. "I arranged Simon so Edwin could see someone he loved the way the Birkenau prisoners were after they were gassed: in a big shovel to be dumped in a mass grave. Like my father."

I searched my racing thoughts for something to say. I had to keep Tony talking. "What about Edwin?"

Tony frowned. "I think you're trying to stall, Meg. You're hoping that boyfriend of yours will swoop in and rescue you. You're forgetting something."

Puzzled, I looked at him.

"There are enough bullets in my gun for Brad and Jon too, Meg." He was right. I hadn't thought of that. Now I willed Brad to stay away and ransacked my mind for ways I could escape.

"So," said Tony, his lips curled in a sneer, "I'll tell you about Edwin Porter."

I nodded, "Please go on."

"That man came to our home. Our home."
Tony said. "He wanted to talk with us about selling our home to his company. I was outside when
I saw his car—that huge, fancy, black automobile
that he and the others drive around in—pulled up
and parked in the driveway. He was alone, and
came up to me. All smiles. Wanted to shake my
hand. I knew him for the evil thing he was. I didn't
want to invite him in, but it was daytime, and…"

"You couldn't very well kill him in your
front yard," I said.

"Good, Meg," Tony said, as if rewarding a
prize pupil in one of his courses. "Quite good.
Mother was napping in the next room. I fixed up
my study as her bedroom a few years ago when
she couldn't manage the stairs any longer. So I
asked Edwin to sit down, which he did—and then
began talking about how wonderful it would be for
Mother and me to live somewhere else, somewhere warm.

"Unfortunately, Mother heard our voices,
and called out to me. I excused myself, and went
over to the door to her room. I opened it, and
Mother screamed, *'Kapo!'* That devil was right

behind me, had followed me to her room. He didn't recognize my mother right away, but he knew what she meant." Tony paused. "Do you know what he did then?"

I shook my head.

"Edwin pushed past me, went over to her, and said, 'Do we know each other from Birkenau?' My mother was frightened. She couldn't speak. But that didn't stop him. He lifted her arm and examined her ID. 'I remember you,' he said. Edwin could see how scared she was, but still wouldn't stop. He went on about how sorry he was that things had happened in the camp, how he tried to intercede with the SS to spare her from the experiments. He asked her to forgive him. Over and over, he asked. He wouldn't stop. He wouldn't stop."

Tony's face was livid, twisted in rage. In the light of the lantern, he looked diabolical. As perhaps he was.

"So I pushed him out of Mother's room. He stood in our parlor, still shouting to her, begging for forgiveness. He wouldn't stop until I hit him again and again with the fireplace poker."

Again, that calm, detached voice, "I looked outside. No one was around. Almost everyone is gone during the day." I thought back. Tony was committing murder while I was napping.

Tony said, "I switched the cars. I couldn't have Edwin's car seen at our house. It was a huge risk, but I had to chance it. I put his car in my garage, and put mine in the driveway. I came back in and rolled Edwin up in the living room rug. I'd moved him as far as the kitchen, when I heard my mother cry out.

"I hurried to her room. She was unconscious, but alive. I called for an ambulance. The paramedics arrived, and I followed the ambulance to the hospital in my car. I stayed with her until the doctors told me that she was resting comfortably, and nothing more could be done that night. They advised me to go home and rest, and come back in the morning." Tony smiled again. "I went home, but I didn't rest."

That must've been about the time that Brad and I came by with food for Tony. Dear God, I remembered thinking how beautiful the hardwood floors were in the room. The faded rose-colored flowered rug covered them when Sally and I were there, but when Brad and I stopped by, the floors were bare. The rug was wrapped around Edwin's body in the kitchen. No wonder Tony was so nervous about my offer to get a rag from the kitchen to wipe up the food we spilled.

Tony smirked. "Now comes the clever part. The police and everyone else thought Simon's death was meant to, shall we say, discourage the building of all those condos and things. So I decided to take Edwin Porter's body to the construction yard and pose him there. I couldn't have any connection made between the two Porters and me. I had to keep Mother safe, and I couldn't do that if I was arrested.

"His automobile was a problem. I couldn't leave it in my garage, and, in any case, I needed it to drive Edwin to the yard. My car's too small. But what could I do with the car after I drove it to the yard? If I left it there, how would I get home?"

"And so you took my kayak," I answered.

"You really are quite bright, Meg," said Tony. "The Lincoln was big enough to hold both the kayak and Edwin, so I drove to the construction yard, put Edwin down outside the gate—such

a disappointment that the yard was locked up—
and paddled your kayak home. I trust you found it
safe and sound?"

"Yes," I said. I didn't want to take a
chance on stirring up his anger by telling him he
left mud and twigs in the kayak, and they fell on
me when I put the boat away for the winter.

Tony mused, "I only made one mistake.
When I turned off the ignition of Porter's car, I
automatically locked the door, and put the keys in
my pocket. I thought for sure you'd noticed the
extra set with the rental car tag in the dish by my
front door."

"No, I didn't."

"No matter." Tony leaned toward me.
"You understand, don't you, Meg? I had to guard
Mother. So much evil…"

I was desperate to keep a conversation going. "How *is* your mother, Tony?" I asked. Wrong
move.

His faced clouded up and he sobbed, "She
passed away not too long after you visited her.
She's gone, Meg. That Evil One killed her. What
will I do without her?" He pounded the table with
his free hand. I couldn't help but notice how pow-

erful his hands and arms were from paddling his heavy old wooden rowboat. In a bizarre deviance from Scheherazade in *One Thousand and One Nights,* I'd postponed my death, but my story had ended. I was out of options.

Chapter 34

"Dear, dear Meg," Tony said. "You are so smart and clever. I like you, but I can't leave you alive to tell this story to the police. You must know that. I must take care of Mother's..."His voice broke. "Burial, her memory."

Panic welled in my throat. If this were a fictional "crazy cat lady" story, Minerva would pounce on Tony, I would seize his gun, and hold him at bay until help arrived. Fat chance. I had no doubt the craven Minerva was crouched under my bed upstairs, her refuge from thunderstorms.

"Stand up and turn around, Meg," Tony said. "It would be easiest for both of us if I put a bullet in the back of your head."

"Perhaps we should go outside to do this. Any, uh, mess would wash away in the rain," I suggested desperately playing for more time. "No one will see us. No one's out in this storm."

Tony stared at me. Under other circumstances, I would find it remarkable that an unhinged person would look at me as if I were the one unhinged.

"One more question?" I asked.

"What? Your stalling won't make this any easier for you."

"What did you do with the rug?"

"It's in my garage," Tony said. "I didn't want to leave it with Edwin's car because it would be traced back to me. Why, do you like it? That's good, because it will be your grave cloth." Tony giggled.

"Stand up, Meg, and face the wall. Now." Tony rose from his chair and came up behind me. I closed my eyes. I thought of all the things I'd left undone, all my intentions, and my family, Brad...

There was a sound of breaking glass, and Tony's gun clattered to the floor. Tony and I scrambled under the table for his weapon. Tony grabbed it.

Someone came through the back door. As Tony stood up, Jon punched him in the face and Tony fell to the floor. When he moved, Jon sat on him. "Don't even think of making any moves, you bastard."

Rubbing his knuckles, Jon said, "Get Tony's gun, Meg. And while you're at it, get Brad's surgical boot."

Brad hobbled in. "Are you all right, Meg?" He limped over and wrapped me in a tight embrace.

I nodded through my sobs. "I thought I'd never…"

"Shh, shh," he said, stroking my hair.

§

After Brad strapped on his surgical boot, he and Jon tied up Tony with a length of rope from my laundry room. I went upstairs and changed into dry clothes, while Brad opened the hall closet and brought out some of his clothes for Jon and himself. Soon we were sitting before a roaring fire and drinking the wine I'd bought at the store that afternoon. Through the doorway, the men kept an eye on Tony.

Brad said to Jon, "Where did you learn to throw a punch like that?"

"Being gay, I was bullied a lot as a kid, so my father took me to a gym, taught me a few moves."

"How did you know I was in trouble?" I asked.

Brad said, "We ran into Sally at the drug store. I had to get a prescription filled for a cream to treat the rash the splint caused on my leg. She mentioned that you'd been at the library looking at concentration camp tattoos. I remembered seeing Edwin Porter's tattoo listed in the reports from the coroner, and I knew that Gita Banicki had also been in a concentration camp."

"But," said Jon, "we had a flat tire. Tony Banicki came roaring by us in his car. We tried to flag him down, but he ignored us. We knew he'd seen us. If he'd been going toward the hospital, that would've been understandable—maybe his mother's condition had changed—but why would he be rushing home?"

"And," said Brad, taking up the account, "when we finally got here, his car was parked in front of your house. All the lights were out, of course, so we snuck up to the kitchen window and looked in. Both of you were facing the wall and didn't see us. Like an idiot, I'd left my weapon here. So, I took off my boot and threw it through the window at him. I was afraid his gun would go off, but he was set to pull the trigger, so I had no choice. Thank God he forgot to take the safety off the gun."

"Good throw," I said.

"Was a quarterback for the Terps," Brad said. "Don't be impressed. I was terrible. Sat on the bench for two years. Guess I finally mastered the bootleg."

Jon and I groaned.

The three of us moved to the living room, where we could watch Tony through the doorway. I heard the kitchen door open, followed by, "Holy shit!"

"Hi, Louis," I called, "come on in."

Louis removed his boots and joined us. "What's going on? Why is Anatole Banicki trussed like a turkey in your kitchen?"

Louis's expression went from incredulous to concerned as we filled him in. "Everyone's okay, right? No one hurt—except for the turkey in the kitchen?" We assured him we were fine. He took his cell phone from his pocket. "No signal. I'll take the car and drive over to the police station, get them over here."

A squad car arrived a little over an hour later. Chief Koenig and the young patrolman I'd met at the police station clumped in. As they listened to our story, Billy said, "Well, I'll be—"

several times. I waited for him to scratch his head in confusion, and I wasn't disappointed.

Brad said, "Chief, can we come down to the station tomorrow and give you our statements? Meg, here, has had a rough time."

"Yeah, sure," Billy said. He and the patrolman got up and walked toward the kitchen.

The rain began to let up and the skies were quiet at long last. Minerva appeared and scampered ahead of the men to the kitchen.

"Stay there, Meg. I'll let everyone out," said Brad, adding with a pointed look in my direction, "and lock up."

Brad was laughing when he returned. "Before they could cuff Tony, Minerva attacked him and gave him a nasty scratch on his face. Seems he was lying on her food dish."

I hoped that didn't make me a crazy cat lady, after all.

Chapter 35

My mother saw a Phoenix television station's news bulletin about Tony Banicki's arrest and telephoned the next day. "Meg, I'm so glad that man is in jail. We worried so much about you."

"All's well, Mom. Nothing more to fret about."

"I was surprised your byline wasn't on the story. Weren't you covering it for the *Journal-Times?*"

"We had no electric power or phone lines here, so I couldn't get anything to Harry Josten in time. The wire service picked it up overnight from the police. I e-mailed a follow-up article to Harry this morning when the power came back on."

"Your Dad and I are all set for Christmas," she said.

"Oh, where will you be?" I asked in all innocence, knowing they weren't visiting me after the blizzard of the previous year.

"We thought we'd spend it with you, dear," Mom said, "but don't go to any work. We're not fussy." It was a good thing Mom couldn't see my eyeballs orbiting their sockets. I jotted down their travel details and chatted a while before we hung up.

I laughed to myself. The power outage did keep me from filing a story last night. A good thing, because the last thing I wanted to do after Brad and I were alone was dash off several paragraphs of deathless prose.

§

After closing the door behind the police and Tony the night before, Brad returned to the living room, sat down beside me on the sofa, and unfastened his boot. Within minutes, we had each other's clothes off and were rolling around on the rug like a pair of crazed minks.

We wrapped ourselves in a blanket and sat for a long while afterward, talking, and sipping the remaining wine. Brad held my face in his hands and said, "I love you, Meg."

"And I love you," I said, holding him tighter.

Drowsiness overcame us, and we walked upstairs to my bedroom. We slept for a while, sought each other's pleasure again, and curled up together in the warmth created by our bodies.

Chapter 36

The Heron was jammed the next night when Brad and I entered the restaurant to meet Sally and Craig for dinner. News of the capture of the murderer and a report in the *Bramble Buzz* that eminent domain was deemed "inadvisable and impractical" by the town council, brought many residents to the Heron to celebrate. The room hummed with conversation and laughter.

Almost all of the Cottage Row residents were there. Jake Tigran came in with Marlene, who looked much better than when I last saw her in the hospital. I meant to visit her, but her mother was staying with her and taking care of the kids while Marlene attended outpatient therapy. Jake's red truck was usually at their house at noon and by dinnertime—one day with a clothes dryer strapped in the truck bed—so it appeared he was making an effort to help Marlene and save their marriage.

While we waited to be seated, Mayor Koenig walked to the microphone on the small dance floor and lifted his pudgy hands to quiet the knot of people that had gathered in front of him. "Many of you asked about the story in the *Buzz* about the Prairie Lake development. There'll be an official announcement sent to your homes next week. Since so many of you are here tonight, without any further adieu, I'd like to call on my lovely wife and village attorney to tell you the details."

Sally poked me in the ribs and gave me a questioning look. "Yes," I whispered, "Fred really said, 'adieu,' and not 'ado.'"

Frieda Koenig, clad in one of her many dun business suits, marched up to the mike. "Hello, everyone. I'll make this short and as simple as I can." With that, she launched into several minutes of complex legalese about eminent domain. The crowd grew restive. Finally, she finished and asked for questions.

"Yeah. What the hell did you just say?" Laughter rippled through the crowd. Pete Winters turned and waved his glass of beer to the audience. Kim tugged at her husband's sleeve and hissed something in his ear.

"Mr. Winters, I see you're right to the point as usual," Frieda twitched her lips in an unsuccessful attempt to smile, as her eyes drew a bead on him. "The village board dropped all plans to seize—uh—acquire by eminent domain, the property known as Cottage Row." Sustained applause erupted.

From a corner of the room, a man called out, "May I say a few words?"

People turned toward the voice, craning their necks to see who had spoken.

Mayor Koenig said, "Why, of course, Mr. Burton. I had no idea you were here."

"Poor man," said Sally, "probably came here for a quiet dinner."

As Travis Burton came forward and joined the Koenigs at the microphone, Mayor Koenig said, "We're now going to hear from Mr. Travis Burton, partner in Porter-Burton Enterprises, but before we do, Travis, I'd like to extend heartfelt sympathies to you and the Porter family from all of us Brambletonians."

Sally gave me another nudge, and raised her eyebrows at me. Brambletonians?

Travis shook Fred's hand, and said, "Thank you, Mr. Mayor." To the assemblage, Travis said, "In addition to the eminent domain situation, Susanne—Mrs. Porter—withdrew her investment in the project, and frankly, I don't have the wherewithal to finance the development alone, that is, without additional investors." He paused. "After the deaths of Simon and Edwin Porter, people who might normally be interested are reluctant to risk their money in the development. For those who aren't here tonight and for others with an interest in the project, a full-page ad will be in the *Chicago Journal-Times* tomorrow, announcing the closure of the Prairie Lake development. The earth-moving equipment and construction trailer at the old lumberyard we've been renting will be hauled away over the next few days." The crowd parted in silence as he strode through the restaurant and out the door.

As the Koenig couple turned to leave the floor, Mr. Trimble from the bank stepped up and spoke quietly with the Mayor.

"We have another person who wishes to speak," said Mayor Koenig, "Our esteemed banker, J. Forrest Trimble the Third." Sporadic clapping.

Trimble patted down the seventeen hairs crossing his pate, and began. "Dear friends, I have some good news tonight. As most of you know, one of the empty houses on Red Fox Lane was rented to Mr. Trinder, Meg Smyth's, er, good friend. He's doing a wonderful job."

Trimble looked bewildered as the crowd laughed and looked over at us. Trimble sure had a way with words. I looked at Brad. Was he blushing?

"But wait! There's more!" I couldn't believe Trimble used the used-car dealer trope. My three dinner companions couldn't either believe it, either. Their shoulders shook with suppressed laughter. Sally and Brad both nudged me. I hoped we'd be seated at a table soon before my ribs were black and blue.

"Our little town was rocked by the terrible things that happened over the last month or so," said Trimble. The audience nodded in assent.

"But every cloud has a silver lining," Trimble continued. I braced for a nudge from Sally at Trimble's platitude, but Sally's elbow remained at her side. "I'm pleased to announce that the Banicki residence has been sold, and the new owner is here with us tonight."

Brad, Sally, Craig, and I looked at each other. We'd assumed that the Banicki house would be empty for a long time, no prospective buyer wishing to purchase a house where a murder had taken place.

A huge smile wreathing his face, Trimble said, "Come on up here, little lady," and motioned to someone perched on a stool in the bar area. Mincing up to the mike and waving to everyone like a beauty contestant on a runway came Gloria. I may have been too hasty in my analogy, in that beauty-queen contestants don't usually chew gum and have purple hair. And they probably do a bit better walking in four-inch heels, but still: Gloria.

As everyone applauded, Brad leaned over and asked, "Who is that?"

"Gloria Morelli. She owns Gloria's Glamour beauty shop," I said, with an exaggerated toss of my head, "and most recently, the creator of my *avant-garde* hairstyle."

Fortunately, Gloria didn't have much to say. She shook Koenig's and Trimble's hands, waved again to all of us, and teetered back to the bar.

"Thank you, Woody," said the Mayor.

Woody? Was that J. Forrest Trimble's nickname? Pokes to my ribs from Sally and Brad. I saw Ben-Gay in my immediate future.

Ben Fulton, wheeling Nina in her wheelchair, came up to us. We walked with him as he wheeled her over to where the Tigrans were standing a bit away from the press of the crowd. "Marlene, dear, I'm so glad to see you," Nina said. "How are you doing?"

"Okay, I guess. Better. I feel like such a fool," Marlene said. She reached up and touched Jake's hand. "Jake's been wonderful. He's even given up chewing tobacco. Well, almost given it up." Jake gave Nina an "aw shucks" grin as Marlene smiled.

"Marlene, we all have things we feel foolish about, things that get us down. The important thing is to get back up. And it looks like you have, dear," Nina said.

"My mother is here now," Marlene said, joining the legion of eye-rollers, "but maybe I could stop in and chat with you sometime after she's not here every day?" Nina, with her near-invalid health, probably fights against frustration and depression a lot. She would be good for Marlene. And I'd bet Marlene would be good for Nina, too.

"Of course, dear, that would be lovely," Nina said.

Ben said, "Marlene, when you're up to it, perhaps you'd like to help us out a few hours a week at the hardware store? I'd like to stay open the afternoons I take Nina to the doctor."

Marlene said, "I'd love that!" She looked at Jake. "What do you think?"

Jake beamed and said, "Fine with me."

§

A sophisticated-looking young woman touched Brad's elbow. "Your table is ready, sir."

I turned. "Babsy Wilcox? Is that you?"

"I decided to go by my full name, 'Barbara,' Ms. Smyth. I'm working here now and," she said with a grin, "I'll be your server this evening." She led us to a booth and handed us menus.

We looked up when we heard the crowd chant, "We want Jon! We want Jon!" News of his punching Tony Banicki and rescuing me had flooded the Bramble's gossip pipeline. Jon, wearing his executive chef's coat, black-checkered pants, and white traditional chef's hat, emerged from the kitchen. He looked pleased and embarrassed. People were clamoring to shake his hand and offering to buy him drinks.

We saw Louis, who stood beaming next to his partner, tense as Pete Winters went up to them. The group grew quiet. Pete made no secret of his opinion of gays. Pete extended his hand to Jon, who reached out and shook it. We all applauded again.

Chapter 37

Pastor Joe was leaving the Heron at the same time we were, so we suggested he join us in a nightcap at the hotel. He accepted our invitation with alacrity. I once asked the pastor about the church's view on drinking, and he quoted Martin Luther. I had it screened on a T-shirt for him: "Whoever drinks beer, he is quick to sleep; whoever sleeps long, does not sin; whoever does not sin, enters Heaven! Thus, let us drink beer!"

After we were settled and served, I asked, "What about PBE, Brad?"

"Between us," he replied, "Porter-Burton Enterprises invested in junk bonds and over-valued dot-com start-ups. I think the dot-com bubble will collapse, and PBE will be ruined. Simon Porter was also engaged in some shady financial deals, possibly laundering money for one of the mobs. That's what brought me here—the money laundering scheme wasn't limited to just one state, and the FBI became quite interested in their tax filings. Craig was a great help."

"What about Travis? Will he be indicted?" asked Sally.

"I'm not sure. It looks, right now, that he

was unaware of Simon's activities. He knew from the start that I'm with the Bureau and has cooperated fully with our investigation. I know Edwin didn't know about it, as he was a figurehead and not involved in the day-to-day business. He tried to help PBE with the Prairie Lake development, and that went terribly wrong, as we know."

"And Susanne?"

Brad laughed. "No surprise there. She dumped PBE and Travis as soon as she returned to Chicago. She's probably got her claws into her next rich guy by now."

"I was surprised about the Banicki house," I said. "I'm not sure I'd want to live in a house where there was a recent murder. Gloria must have nerves of steel."

"She probably got a wonderful deal," Craig said. "It's an empty old house and in foreclosure."

"I hope someone buys the house next to me sometime soon," I said. "I hate to see it standing empty and deteriorating."

Pastor Joe traced the condensation on the outside of his beer stein with his finger. "Such sad lives Tony and Gita Banicki lived."

"Tony's mother and Edwin Porter were prisoners at Auschwitz-Birkenau, weren't they?" Sally asked.

"Yes, and when Porter showed up here, she was terrified," I said. "Porter had been a *kapo,* kind of like a 'trusty' in a prison."

Brad said, "I looked through the Bureau's lists of *kapos* whose atrocities classified them as war criminals," Brad said. "Edwin's name wasn't listed among the people being sought."

"Edwin seems to have led an exemplary life since the war. He's been generous in giving to a number of Jewish charities, especially ones assisting Holocaust survivors and their families," I said, recalling the clippings from the *Journal-Times*.

"Guilt, perhaps," Brad said. "But guilt about his brutality to others, or guilt because he survived the brutality?"

Pastor Joe said, "Tony surely felt guilty too—growing up Jewish without fear, an Oxford education, good friends—while his parents endured unimaginable horrors."

"There's no doubt Gita Banicki was terrified at a specter of the past invading the safety of her life and home," I said. "There's a question there, too: was it Edwin himself who terrified her, or was it the awful memories his presence brought to her confused mind?"

"It didn't matter to Tony if Edwin was a vicious *kapo* or one who was a victim of circumstance in that unspeakable camp," Brad said. "It was all about shielding his mother. And in the end, he lost his bearings and his mind to his obsession."

"The greatest atrocity of all," Pastor Joe said, "is that Tony fought evil with evil."

We sipped our drinks.

Craig broke the silence. "Meg, did Brad tell you his news?"

"Craig!" Sally lasered a look at him.

I looked at Brad. "What news?" I asked.

"I asked the Bureau for a transfer," Brad said.

The bottom dropped out of my stomach. He's a wanderer. He said so himself. He has no roots, no home. I steeled myself and forced a bright smile, "Oh? Where to?"

"Chicago." Brad grinned. "There was an opening, and I went in this morning and talked with the Bureau chief about it. It's a permanent assignment. Still some travel and I'd have to commute to the Loop once or twice a week."

"Commute?" I asked. "From here?"

"Nope," Brad teased, "from Ocean View, Iowa."

It's not often I'm speechless, but this was one of those times. We'd talked about the future off and on during his stay at my house, but I didn't dare hope. I didn't know how to ask now where he would be living. He saved me by saying, "I've an option to buy the house I'm renting on Cottage Row. It needs a lot of work, but after I live there a while, I'll have a better idea as to whether it's worth buying."

I was both thrilled and relieved. Neither Brad nor I was ready for the commitment of getting married, or even living together. Having him close was a happy compromise. I squeezed his arm. "Oh, Brad, I'm so glad."

"What about you, Meg?" asked Sally. "Do you have an itch to go back to investigative reporting?"

"Are you kidding?" I asked. "This was enough for me. I came here to get away from murders and violence. I've had enough excitement to last me a long, long time. I'll be glad to get back to being Miss Polly, although Harry did assign me to do a series on how a small town plans to celebrate the millennium. It doesn't seem possible it's coming up in a little over a year. I remember when the year 2000 was when science-fiction stories took place."

"Depends," said Craig, "if we're celebrating the 'odometer turn' from 1999 to 2000, or the real millennium, from 2000 to 2001."

"Craig!" said Sally. She smiled and shook her head.

"What?" he asked, looking a bit bewildered.

Before Craig could launch into myriad details, I said, "The *Journal* opted for January 1, 2000, as the beginning of the next century."

"Maybe you can offer a photo op to Max Trent, decked out in his Statue of Liberty outfit," Sally said with a laugh.

"I think not," I said.

Acknowledgments

With sincere and ongoing appreciation to:

My family and friends, whose affection and support strengthen me daily in so many ways;

Holly Love, proofreader extraordinaire;

Ralph Love, Sarajoy Pickholtz, and Cathy Konczyk for giving freely of their expertise and encouragement;

The Barrington Writers Workshop, whose members cheered me on with their comments and gentle suggestions and corrections.

About the Author

Julie Kendrick started her writing career as a journalist with a daily newspaper in the Chicago area. She was managing editor of a scientific and engineering journal, and served on the boards of directors of several not-for-profit organizations. She sings with an international award-winning *a-cappella* women's chorus.

An outdoor photographer, she travels extensively, most recently from "Pole to Pole"—Greenland to the Antarctic.

Fatal Development is her first novel. More mystery adventures are planned for Meg Smyth and the residents of Bramble.